T0160847

PASTURE ART

ALSO BY MARLIN BARTON

The Cross Garden
Dancing by the River
A Broken Thing
The Dry Well

PASTURE ART

STORIES BY MARLIN BARTON

HUB CITY PRESS
SPARTANBURG, SC

First printing: March 2015
Cover and Book Design: Meg Reid
Proofreader: James Yeh
Copy editor: Jan Scalisi
Printed in Dexter, MI by Thomson-Shore
Cover Photo © Robert Richard

Library of Congress Cataloging-in-
Publication Data

Barton, Marlin, 1961-
  [Short stories. Selections]
  Pasture art : stories and a novella / by Marlin
Barton.
      pages ; cm
  ISBN 978-1-938235-09-2 (softcover : acid-free
paper)--ISBN 978-1-938235-10-8 (ebook)
  1. Alabama--Social life and customs--Fiction.
I. Title.
  PS3552.A7727A6 2015
  813'.54--dc23

 HUB CITY
PRESS

186 West Main St.
Spartanburg, SC 29306
1.864.577.9349

www.hubcity.org
www.twitter.com/hubcitypress

for Mike Smith
and friendship long-term,

and for the Phillips family of Forkland, Alabama,
four generations of friendship

CONTENTS

PASTURE ART

THE HELICOPTER SITS IN THE MIDDLE of the hay field, its blades still except when the wind blows. Just beyond it a sailboat rides crashing waves, and the train engine strains up the small rise, though its smokestack never blows smoke. There are giant bugs, too, and spiders, a matador with red cape in front of a charging bull, and a tank with its cannon raised. A huge baseball cap with an A for the Atlanta Braves sits at the edge of the field, two eyes just beneath the brim. It isn't lost on Leah that her three favorites are all something she can ride away on. Out of here by water, rail, or air—any way will do.

Pasture art, that's what Mr. Hutchins calls it. Leah guesses he knows what he's talking about. After all, he's the one who makes it, and it is his pasture, just like it's his tenant house they rent and his old car they make payments on. She's read about indentured servants in history class. That's what she feels like. Cleaning his house and cooking for him three times a week doesn't help with that feeling, either.

He mostly uses round bales when he works on his creations, and she's watched him move hay with the large fork on the front of his tractor. But he'll use anything that works: cut-up pieces of tin, rusty fifty-five gallon drums, driftwood from out of the Tennahpush River, a mirror he took from an old house that had fallen in, which is what he used for the door on the helicopter. Long pieces of tin make the 'copter's blades, and old drums welded to a galvanized pipe form its tail and back rudder. When she squints it looks almost real, as if it might lift, hover, and be gone.

"A waste of good hay," her mother says from behind her. "And to think, people come out to take pictures of it."

Leah turns away from the window and finds her mother leaning against the kitchen doorway for support. She has bad feet, the bottom of one bruised over for more than two weeks now.

"I like looking at all of it," Leah says.

"I don't know why. Looks like something a child would do."

"It's different," she says.

"It's hay and junk is what it is."

Leah isn't going to argue. "Time for your shot," she says, which is its own argument, but one she feels she has to wage.

Her mother shakes her head and waves a hand through the air dismissively. Maybe it's the slight roll of her eyes, the way a girl would, or the way she turns her head in a teenager's defiance, but for a moment Leah catches a glimpse of her mother as she must have looked when she was Leah's age. Leah has seen pictures and knows that, unlike herself, her mother had been pretty once, but that was before two husbands had left her, and now a third, it appears, before she'd worked waitress and factory jobs, before she'd started to drink, and before they found out she'd been sick for years and didn't know it.

"If we don't keep your blood sugar down, you'll get ketoacidosis again."

"Why do you always use doctor words? Why don't you call it what it was?"

"All right. It'll keep you from going into a coma again. That plain enough for you?"

Leah walks past her mother and gets the vial of insulin out of the refrigerator. After she draws the right number of units, her mother lifts her shirt and Leah makes the injection into a small roll of pinched fat on her stomach right between two small bruises.

"You could do this yourself," she says. "You ought to. They showed you how."

"And deny you the pleasure?"

"If you don't take better care of yourself, they'll end up taking your foot off. I guess I'll have to do everything then."

"Guess you will. You can rule the roost. Won't you like that?"

It's moments like these that make Leah's mind sail away across hay-bale waves and over the field of an old man's imagination. But to where? It seems her own imagination is too far out of reach.

She pulls the rusty Lincoln around to the back of the house and catches sight of the buck and doe that stand always at the edge of the high bank above the Tennahpush. Each statue is riddled with bullet holes on the river side. "You wouldn't think so many fishermen carried high powered rifles," Mr. Hutchins once said, "or that their eyesight was so bad they couldn't tell fur from painted concrete, even with a scope."

She'd wanted to tell him their eyesight was fine, that shooting those two deer had become a regular sport up and down the river. She knew Mosler, her second, and now maybe final, stepfather, had taken some shots at them, and so had some of the men who'd worked for Hutchins, men he'd fired.

Now Mosler is gone, cutting pulpwood down around Brewton. He quit the paper mill and left not long after her mother came home from the hospital. For six months, he sent money, but then it stopped coming, along with any word from him. At least Mosler's health insurance at the mill had covered the hospital bills, or most of them. But now, with him gone, there is no way she and her mother can keep making rent and car payments, to say nothing of the drug-store bills. She wants to be angry at Mosler, but can't, and won't let herself think too hard about why.

The old man's truck is gone, but she lets herself in and closes the heavy door behind her. When he first gave her a key, she didn't think anything about it, but later she decided that either he was more trusting than he ought to be or was so full of himself he never stopped to think someone might actually steal from him.

She cleans his bathroom first, and the smell of cleanser feels as if it's scraping away the insides of her lungs. She hates this part of her job, doesn't want to clean someone else's commode. Maybe that's why her taking began here in this bathroom. Months ago, she opened a drawer, saw the brightly colored extra toothbrushes still in their plastic wrappers, and slipped one into her pocket. Such a simple thing. Afterward, each item she took grew larger and more expensive, and nothing she's taken lately, not the silver tea tray out of the sideboard or the porcelain figurine from the guest bedroom, would fit into something so small as a pocket. She tells herself that she's going to sell everything she's taken, but she hasn't yet.

She hears him now, coming in the back door. He doesn't call out to her. He never does, and she wonders if he likes knowing someone else is already inside. Maybe he pretends, just for a moment, that his wife is still alive, waiting for him to come home. She's tried to imagine being someone's wife but somehow can't picture any kind of a husband for herself, not out of the boys she knows in her summer school classes, and her mind doesn't seem capable of moving beyond them, as if her choices are always limited to only what she knows in the present.

He is in the kitchen when she finds him, has taken off his hat, and his gray hair stands out around his ears. She knows he doesn't care, and she envies this somehow. She feels like her own hair and clothes never look right, or even her smile, and though she pretends not to care about these things, she can't completely deny to herself that she does.

"I'll start your supper in a little while," she says.

"No need. Not tonight."

She stands there, not moving.

"It's all right. I'll still pay you for the same amount of time."

She shrugs her shoulders.

He watches her for a moment. "So are you saving any of what I'm paying you?"

Maybe he's only trying to make conversation, but she can't believe the rudeness of his question.

"Yeah, I take my check to the grocery store every week in Demarville and they hold it for me, let me have the groceries for free."

He looks away, embarrassed, not for himself, she realizes, but for her. Before her mother went to the hospital, she wouldn't have spoken this way. Maybe that's why he forgives her, she guesses, and doesn't snap back, or fire her. Or maybe an old man whose wife is dead only four months just doesn't have the energy to get angry.

By way of apology, she changes the subject, softens her tone. "You haven't made anything new in a good while, Mr. Hutchins."

For a moment he looks puzzled and seems to have no idea what she's talking about. Then understanding registers on his face. "No, I haven't," he says finally. "No hay creatures or anything else since Charlotte died."

She'd never made the connection—that his wife's death ended his work in the pasture. She suddenly feels worse now than she did for her remark about her check. "I'm sorry. I hadn't..."

"It's all right. Seems like her death took everything with it, like it even stole away with things right out of the house." He's looking squarely at her, and she doesn't have to wonder too hard about what he's trying to say. She waits for it, braces herself, but he doesn't make a direct accusation. He only sits there.

"I've still got to dust your bedroom and the living room," she says, not sure what other words to offer up. Somehow even her conscience feels mute, as if she can't square the reality of being caught with the wrongness of what she's been doing.

She finds the dust spray and rag where she left them on his bedside table and works from one piece of furniture to another. She can't take anything more, she knows, and wonders what else he might say or do, and when. But still she finds herself opening a drawer here and there, keeping her ear toward the door in case he comes walking down the hall. In the top dresser drawer, she sees several old black and white pictures, all unframed, and while she knows who the serious young bride and groom must be, the woman wearing a beautiful gown, the man in what looks like a naval uniform, they also seem as if they could be any young couple, with hopes for themselves that are bound to come true.

After finishing the bedroom and living room, she puts her cleaning supplies away and hopes to say a quick goodbye. He's sitting at the kitchen table writing a check. When he hands it to her she simply thanks him.

He nods. "Some fresh bullet holes on my two deer. Noticed them earlier today. Reckon how many times concrete deer can die?"

"Maybe it's not fisherman at all," she says.

He makes sure to catch her eye before she can turn away. "Leah, I never really thought it was. Maybe I know a little more about why people do things than you think I do." He speaks quietly, quiet enough that she knows she doesn't have to have to respond, and is grateful for that.

Outside in the car, she's careful not to flood the engine, and the Lincoln finally starts on the third try. She unbuttons her shirt near her waist then and reaches in and feels the slick finish of the photograph against her skin.

The roofline of the two-story house has fallen into a roughly shaped V, but there are rooms on the lower level that stay dry. She gambled. Over a year ago, he took out the few pieces of broken-down furniture that had remained. Now the house sits empty on a corner of his property, at the end of a long dirt road that passes over two cattle guards.

It's almost dark, so she has to hurry. Two days ago, she stole dresses out of the guest bedroom closet, put them in the trunk of the car under an old blanket, and now needs to hide them. She wonders why she risked keeping them in the car this long.

She walks up the crumbling brick steps, carrying the dresses on their wooden hangers. There is no door to open and she enters the large front hall and walks into what must have once been a parlor. Everything she's taken, from toothbrushes to expensive linens to shoes to cookware, lies piled, as neatly as possible, in the middle of the room, away from windows with missing panes. She drapes the dresses across the pile and is about to walk away when she looks down at the long black dress on top and feels compelled to touch the voile and run her fingers along the thin straps and deep neckline. She wonders when Mrs. Hutchins had ever had a chance to wear it and feels as if it must have been made for some special event, but she can't imagine what that might have been.

The dress makes her aware of her own body. She feels the thin sheen of sweat trapped by her jeans and T-shirt and the tightness of the elastic in her bra and underwear. She dares herself then.

The button on her jeans is tight. She works it loose and pushes her jeans down and steps out of them. Already her entire body feels cooler. She pulls off her T-shirt and slips out of her bra. Her blood feels as if it's running more quickly through her, and she feels a tightness in her legs and arms in contrast to the softness of her belly beneath her hands. She pulls the dress over herself and pushes it into place. It's somewhat tight across her hips, and the coarseness of the material feels like fine sandpaper against the softest points of her body. Beyond these sensations, she isn't sure how she feels. She looks down at herself and slides her hands across her stomach, pushes them down her hips and then legs. She feels as if she is searching for someone inside the dress, someone she might be or could become. She wishes for a mirror that would show her what she can't envision for herself, one that would take her beyond the sweating body she looks down on. A mirror once hung somewhere in this house, and she knows where it is now, on the side of a helicopter made out of hay, tin, and empty drums, all pieced together out of an old man's vision that he can't find his way to any longer.

She looks down at herself again and feels some sense of failure that maybe they have both come to share, and she sees then what isn't there in the pile she has collected for so many months now, the silver tea tray that had been sitting on top of the linens. It is gone, along with the gold necklace she'd left curled in the center of the tray's intricately cut design.

Her house is dark, but she isn't afraid of what she'll find inside. Routine has killed her fears.

The television is on with the sound turned down, and her mother sleeps at a twisted angle on the low-slung sofa. Or if she isn't asleep exactly, the words *passed out*, Leah tells herself, are too strong. At least she hopes they are. She wakes her mother without much effort. "Did you eat anything first? You know when you drink and don't eat, you get hypoglycemic." Her mother keeps blinking her eyes. "Then I have to shoot you with the glucagon, bring you back."

"From what? The dead? I ain't died yet. And I did eat, if you want to know."

"I don't know if I believe that. I guess you think you're as hard to kill as those deer Mr. Hutchins has standing on the riverbank."

Her mother turns away and faces the back of the sofa. Her words come muffled. "The only person shoots me is you."

"But that's to keep you alive and healthy."

"Is it?"

Leah doesn't attempt a reply. She goes in the kitchen and comes back with cold cornbread and what her mother still calls sweet milk.

In the morning, she's surprised to hear her mother up earlier than normal, and then even more surprised to see her wearing the nicest dress she has left.

"I'm taking you to school. I need the car this morning."

"How come?"

"I got denied disability. The letter came a couple of days ago. I'm going to talk to a lawyer."

"You aren't disabled. I told you they'd deny it. You can work. You just won't."

Her mother shakes her head and begins to walk out of the small living room, then turns around and faces Leah. "I've worked more years than you've been alive. Pulled double shifts to keep you in diapers and to take up the slack when a man left. Don't tell me what I won't do. I'm tired. I can't stay on my feet like I used to."

"You could quit drinking and take better care of yourself," she says, but even as she says the words she can't imagine they are worth anything.

Summer school lets out at one-thirty. She stands in the parking lot, waiting in the heat waves that rise from the dark, newly poured asphalt, the heat as numbing as the three classes she's just sat through. But she's passing, and by summer's end will be done with it all, graduated, if not exactly with honors. And then what?

She watches the rusty Lincoln pull in and hears the brakes announce its stop. Her mother doesn't move from behind the wheel, so Leah gets in the passenger side and remembers to slam the door hard. One look at her mother's firmly set jaw tells her things didn't go well with the lawyer.

"So what did he say?"

"You should be a lawyer."

"Why is that?"

"Because he told me exactly what you already told me."

"I'm sorry," she says, and in some ways she is. Her mother pulls the heavy car out into the light traffic. "Did you ask him about anything else?"

"Like what?"

"A divorce. Abandonment would be grounds."

"There you go putting big words in your mouth."

"They're not that big. I'm just saying, since he ran out on you, he'd have to pay up. Once they find him."

"And who is they? Who's going to go look for him?"

"I don't know, the law?"

"Ain't no law for us."

They are headed out of town now, the Tennahpush River coming up on her mother's side of the car. Leah wonders what might be floating on its muddy surface or hidden in its depths that Mr. Hutchins could use, some twisted tree trunk maybe, a piece of a rusted-out car.

"Maybe you ought to see about getting food stamps."

"That's where I went after I left the lawyer's office."

What about the employment office? she wants to ask, but doesn't.

In a little while she sees the baseball cap and beyond it the hay creatures—the bugs and spiders and charging bull—that look as if they might walk out of the field and climb over the barbed-wire fence on their twisted spindly legs. Finally she sees the sailboat, the train engine, and the helicopter, all waiting to be boarded.

"So how was school?" her mother asks as they turn onto the dirt road and bounce over the first cattle guard.

The question surprises her, and there's something in her mother's tone she isn't yet sure how to read. "It's fine," she says. "I'm passing, if that's what you mean."

"I guess that is what I mean. What else?" she says, and Leah now sees on her mother's face the same thing she's heard in her voice. It isn't so hard to identify. Leah has been filled with it herself from the moment Mr. Hutchins spoke to her in his kitchen and made clear he knew what she was doing, and the feeling hasn't left her.

That evening she studies for a history test, but it's difficult for her to stay focused. She keeps trying to see her future as her past—written down in a book for her to look back at and understand from some distant present. She wonders how many chapters her life will be worth, but the most she can imagine are blank pages with dates and years written across the top in her own plain hand.

When she wakes in the night she hears the television playing too loudly. At first she tries to ignore it, then wonders how her mother can stand watching the old wooden console while it shouts commercials at her. After another moment, she realizes that her mother isn't watching, or sleeping through the noise. Leah slips out of bed and goes quickly to the kitchen. This isn't routine, but it's happened before. She picks up the small plastic case and hurries into the living room. Her mother's body lies in the dim light from the television, an empty glass overturned on the floor beside her. The clock above the console shows quarter after three. Her mother probably drank for hours, maybe since Leah put away her history book and turned out her bedroom light. Either her mother has slid off the sofa or fallen. She shakes her hard, but there's no response. Now she opens the plastic case, prepares the glucagon, and draws it into the syringe. Her hands are steady and she rolls her mother onto her back. Leah pulls up her mother's shirt, jabs the needle in, and pushes the plunger down.

She waits and her hands begin to tremble the way her mother's sometimes do when there isn't enough energy left in her blood. Her body remains still, and Leah thinks finally to feel for a heartbeat. It's there. And she begins to stir. At first she mumbles words Leah can't understand. Then she seems to see Leah.

"You want something to eat now?" Leah says.

"I don't think so."

"Why do you do things like this?" she asks, but she knows her mother won't answer.

"I think I'm going to be sick."

Leah runs to get the small plastic garbage can out of the bathroom but hears her mother vomiting behind her and stops, not sure whether to move forward or backward.

She takes her history test and decides she has answered enough questions correctly to at least pass, and driving home she thinks about other questions, the ones Mr. Hutchins is bound to ask. Are there any right answers? She has her own questions, too, but no right to ask them, she knows. Still, they've stayed in her mind. Did he see her take something, or did he realize something was missing and suspect her? Maybe he went to the old house for some reason and stumbled across everything.

She is wrong, though. That night at his house, after she's finished her cleaning chores, she browns some pork chops and fries the squash that he bought off a produce truck in town. Before she began cleaning, though, and before he came home, she looked in the sideboard and found the silver tray in the exact place from where she'd taken it, and the gold necklace lay inside the jewelry box that sits on his wife's dresser.

While the pork chops cook in the oven, he comes in and sits at the table, waiting, and asks her nothing. Eventually she decides that maybe he isn't waiting on the food, but on her.

"When do you finish school, Leah?" he finally asks.

"In August." She answers quickly and keeps her back to him.

"Have you thought about what you're going to do then?"

"I've tried to." She knows he must be watching her, but she still can't face him. "Maybe I'll try to get some kind of full-time job in town, in some store, help Mama as much as I can."

She expects a comment from him, but he remains quiet, which is unsettling and feels like a judgment against her—not for stealing from him, though, but for some other kind of failure.

A timer buzzes on the stove, and she turns toward him. He starts to speak, but she can't wait. She shuts her eyes and feels she's about to step off the riverbank beyond the two deer, or fall perhaps, as if shot. "Mr. Hutchins, did you just not want the rest of it? That why you left it all where it was?"

He looks past her for a moment, and seems to give her question careful thought. "Maybe so," he says, softly. "Maybe that is why I left it. And maybe I hoped you wouldn't notice what I'd taken, which might not make much sense to you."

It doesn't. He should be angry, and the fact that he isn't keeps her off balance, uneasy. She wonders if he's playing some game with her. Maybe he's called the sheriff and wants to leave most of the evidence where it is.

"Strange as it may sound," he says, "I felt a little like I was stealing from you."

"Why?" she says, more unsettled than ever.

"I'm not sure. Maybe because I know you must be desperate to do it, and need those things more than me. Or maybe because most of what I saw were my wife's things, not mine. But the tea tray, it had been my mother's, and the necklace was something I bought Charlotte for a wedding anniversary. I couldn't let loose of those things, even though they ought to belong to a woman. The rest of it, maybe I should have already sold or given away."

"I'm sorry," she says, and though she means them, the words don't seem to mean anything when she hears herself say them. He doesn't appear to want or expect an apology. "I'll bring it all back," she adds. What else can she say?

He ignores this, or is too lost in his thoughts to pay her any mind.

"What are you going to do with it? If I can ask."

She feels thrown again. How can he not ask? "I kept telling myself I was going to sell it, to a pawn shop, I guess."

"Because you need money?"

"Of course."

"Money for what?"

"Groceries, rent. What else?"

"But you were hiding it all for yourself, weren't you? Not just from me, but from your mother too. You know I haven't asked your mother for rent in two months."

"No, I didn't know that. She hadn't told me."

"Maybe you don't know why you took it all. Some people steal, Leah. Steal things they don't need. Maybe you just don't know what to do with yourself now that it's time."

"Time for what?"

"That's the question, isn't it? Your question."

"But I don't understand. I don't..."

"You know what you have to do, and maybe that's why I left everything where it was. So I wouldn't interfere with whatever plan you have."

She wishes she had a plan, or that someone would give her one. She turns slowly back to the stove and realizes the timer's buzzing has stopped. She isn't sure for how long.

The night air, hot and dry, pours in through the Lincoln's open window as she follows the curve of the dirt road. It was the Lincoln that gave her away. She asked him before she left, and he told her he saw the tire tracks headed down the road toward the old house and knew he hadn't been through there in weeks. He'd checked them out.

She drives up the small rise and approaches the pasture art from behind. Her lights sweep across several of the creatures, and then she sees a glow beyond her beams that seems out of place and wrong somehow. She knows it isn't from any vehicle out on the highway. The glow grows larger and finally she recognizes it for what it is. The hay-bale body of the train engine blows smoke and flames above its stack. For a moment it seems as if the engine has come to life and, unable to move along any tracks, has exploded into fire.

At first she isn't sure what to do. She stops the car, decides there's no way for her to fight the flames, and turns the Lincoln around. When she pulls up to the house, she's already honking the horn, and he comes hurrying, awkwardly, out the door, his movements slowed by age and maybe arthritis.

"What's wrong?" he says when he reaches her window. She sees from his expression that he's worried for her and wonders if this is what daughters get from their fathers.

"There's a fire," she says, and then explains.

He goes quickly into the house and comes back out with the fire extinguisher that sits in a corner of the kitchen. He puts it in his truck bed, runs as best he can to a small storage house, and emerges with a shovel and hoe.

"Get in the truck with me," he says.

He drives fast, bouncing across ruts, and she finds herself envisioning a grass fire out of control, burning the whole field along with all of his creatures and creations, and already heading toward her house where her mother lies passed out or unconscious. She can't stop herself from imagining terrible visions, and feels not dread but growing excitement.

The flames look higher now, and he leaves the road, heads out across the field, and comes to a stop maybe thirty yards from the burning engine. They climb out of the truck. He grabs the extinguisher and shovel, she gets the hoe, and they move toward the flames.

"We've got to keep it in check, not put out the whole thing," he says, but he doesn't have to tell her. She sees there's no way to put it out, although the fire hasn't grown very wide, which is somehow a disappointment to her.

"Won't it spread?" she asks and begins chopping at small flames in the grass without being told.

"If the ground was any drier, we'd have a hell of a fight on our hands. We might still." He sprays a large patch of flames, then another. "Sparks are going to rain down behind us and all over. Keep your eyes open."

The smokestack and engine cab are gone now, disappeared into a pure heat that seems to penetrate her skin and enter her body, igniting her blood. She looks up and around herself, searching for more fire. The helicopter sits idly, no wind, thankfully, stirs its blades, the only flames there merely reflection. No creatures are suddenly bathed in light. But she sees a small burning on ocean waves that glows against a tapered hull.

He sees it too and motions to her. "Take it," he says and holds out the extinguisher. "You can run faster than me."

She drops the hoe and in a moment is walking across waves, fighting for balance in the straw whitecaps, and sprays the burning water with foam. When she turns, the field, for one moment, is all dark ocean before her with creatures either swimming or floating for survival.

She runs back and reclaims her hoe, giving him the extinguisher. "Good that it's night," he says, "or we'd have a time seeing the flames pop up so quick."

They follow the circular fire-line in opposite directions, and she rises up from time to time, searching for bright flashes among all the strange shapes that now somehow give shape to the whole field.

Eventually they work their way around to each other with the hoe and shovel, sometimes having to stop and put out the small fires behind them. Finally they stand resting, leaned against the wooden handles and watch still for flames that might erupt anywhere, mocking all their efforts.

"Somebody must have set it," she says through thick drifting smoke. "It didn't just start."

"Somebody went from shooting concrete deer to burning up hay locomotives, you think? Maybe so, but this piece was the oldest, the first one I made. Been here for years. A round bale sits long enough, it starts rotting from the inside."

"I don't follow what you mean."

"Rot causes heat," he says and looks at her in the light from the burning mound of hay. "You can't know it's there until it shows itself. Lucky thing you saw it."

"I guess," she says, almost proud of herself, but not quite.

Another sheet of smoke blows between them. "What happened here is pretty rare," he says, "that is if it wasn't somebody's meanness—which isn't rare at all."

She picks up her hoe, jabs it down in a patch of burn. The words are hard for her to say, but she says them. "What I did to you was meanness, wasn't it?"

"I think you know better than that."

She isn't so sure. She remembers then the picture she took, still hidden in the glove compartment of the car, sees him in his uniform and her with her veil lifted, the way they seem to be looking into their future, certain that there's one to look into. She'll have to give this back, will have to hand it to him, try to explain herself, and hope it wasn't meanness.

The fire still burns but seems to only consume itself now. "I'll have to tear down some of the oldest ones," he says, as if to himself.

"Why?"

"If this came from rot, it could happen again."

"You can build them back, though, can't you?"

He doesn't answer for a moment. "I could but don't know if I want to." He leans more heavily against the shovel. "It's hard to make something out of nothing."

"But you've done it. You've taken junk and dead grass and made helicopters."

He looks away. "We better try and shovel some dirt over the burn now. Dig to where the dirt's cooler. We won't have to worry about any more sparks coming down."

As she works her arms become heavier and heavier, and she's surprised that he's able to cover more ground than her.

He drives out of the field, but instead of following the road to his house he drives in the opposite direction. "You need to check on your mother," he says. "She probably saw the fire, wonders where you are. Then I'll take you back to your car."

"I doubt she saw anything," she says and doesn't comment any further.

When he pulls up into the small yard, he simply says, "I'll wait," as if he knows he might embarrass her by going inside.

She finds what she thought she would, her mother sprawled, passed out, on the sofa, or maybe she's only asleep this time. One look in the kitchen and she sees the mostly empty bottle on the counter, and there's no sign at all of her having eaten anything.

After walking back into the living room, she kneels down beside her mother and starts to reach out and shake her, to see if she'll awaken. How hard she has to shake will tell her what she needs to know. But the glucagon kit she used the night before is the last one they had on hand. There is orange juice, though, if she can only rouse her enough to swallow, and if she needs it.

She touches her mother's arm, and with the touch realizes how much heat her own skin still holds, as if its source isn't from outside her body but from within, slowly radiating out of some spot of disintegration or decay that has existed there too long. She lets go of her mother then, stands and presses her hands together, and feels a doubling heat captured within her closed palms.

Outside, in the truck, he asks how her mother is. "I think she's asleep," she says. It's all she offers in answer. She closes her palms together again, presses hard and feels a burning there still, as if she can carry it away with her if only her grasp remains tight enough. Out of that pressure and heat she somehow manages to forage a shape of her own and needs, she finds, to give it to him.

"A dragon," she says into the dark and quiet of the cab. "That's what you should make, a hay dragon, spitting red-tin fire."

He takes a moment before speaking, perhaps needing time to open himself to the vision. "I can see it," he says. "Tell me, what else do you see?"

She thinks a moment, looks at the open field, and there are ocean waves stretching out before her, miles of them, carrying her so deep into imagination that she can taste the burn of salt on her tongue.

BRAIDED LEATHER

THE LENGTH OF BRAIDED LEATHER lay on the table, still wound into a small coil, the same way it hung on the peg beside a stall in the barn. He knew she'd stolen it, and would have to sneak back with it before first light, after she'd cleaned and oiled the tight braids.

He could hear the children playing outside, calling to each other, his daughter's voice high pitched, his son's a little lower. He wondered if he would have remembered their voices if he hadn't seen them again. He'd kept thinking about them, and his wife, when he was hiding.

She was waiting now, down on her hands and knees, her dress pulled not up but down to her waist. In the candlelight the skin of her back was dark and smooth, a way his wasn't and never would be again.

He'd showed her the small cave above the Tennahpush River two weeks before, and she'd helped him store food and water inside, enough for four days. How you gon' send for us? she kept asking. That first night, his dark skin became the darkness inside the white limestone walls—all that whiteness surrounding him, and he felt as if he were disappearing into his freedom.

The next day, long before noon, they came. There hadn't been any dogs, not a single bark or howl. That's how he knew who'd sent them. His hands had shaken with an anger so strong he wanted to fill the air with his own howl. They used the long leather with the nine loose braids at the end, the one they kept locked up in the tack room with the best saddles. It was his first, and all the worse because they'd never expected such a thing from him. Neither had she, he reckoned.

She was waiting still, quietly begging in a low voice. The smell of the meal she'd cooked earlier hung in the room, but the heat from the cook fire had mostly escaped through the open door and windows. He moved to the table, and she grew silent with his steps. He picked up the small coil of leather, ran it through his hands, which shook as he felt the length of it, and measured out how much he would need to give her her freedom, and to take his, again.

INTO SILENCE

FROM WHERE SHE SAT AT the end of the porch she noticed a tall man walking toward her house. The sight of a stranger in Riverfield always raised curiosity, and strangers did come through with some regularity these days, looking for work they knew they wouldn't find or for food they hoped they'd be offered. They were lost men, lost from family and friends, and the closest they could come to home was someone else's doorstep.

This man, though, wasn't walking alone, and to see her mother walking beside him struck her as a little odd. She'd never been one to offer help to those passing through. The faces that held hunger and want didn't seem to move her beyond a concern for herself and her daughter, two women alone.

As they neared the house, she saw how small her mother looked beside him. And yet it wasn't just his height that rendered her mother so small. There was some other dimension to him. Maybe it was his carriage or something in his demeanor that she'd see or feel more clearly when they were closer.

Soon they stood at the steps, and she saw the angular lines of his face and his sharp eyes examining, shifting from one point to another, taking in the house, and her. Then her mother was talking, out loud, not with her hands. "Janey, this is Mr. Clark. I met him up at Anderson's store. He's going to take a look at the room under the stairs."

Her mother spoke too slowly and carefully, so that Janey could be sure to read each word as it was said. She had told her mother many times that she didn't have to do this, but her mother almost always did. When they were in front of people Janey didn't have to hear how it must have sounded to be embarrassed.

Mr. Clark looked at her and nodded but didn't speak. She saw one thing clearly about him now. He wasn't one of those lost men that traveled through. His clothes were clean and fit him well, and his hat, which he removed to reveal a mixture of dark and graying hair cut close, looked almost new. The shirt he wore was neatly pressed, the sleeves rolled up just high enough to show muscular forearms. He'd come here for some purpose. She saw that. She wondered if her mother knew what.

He kept looking at Janey, intently, but not staring. His eyes were a dark brown, like creek water that ran through rich soil. She grew uncomfortable after a moment. Maybe, because of the way her mother had spoken, he suspected she was deaf. It would be like her mother not to have mentioned it. Perhaps he was waiting to see if she'd speak so that he could confirm his suspicion. She simply left her silence open to interpretation.

"Will you show him the room?" her mother said.

She nodded again, stood, and then turned so that he would follow her. The front door opened into a small entrance hall. To the left, narrow stairs wound their way up to the second story, which they didn't use, and to the right was the door that opened into the living room and the rest of the house. Directly ahead and beneath a portion of the stairs was a single bedroom that didn't connect to any other room. Her mother had rented it off and on the last few years when money had become too tight. She hadn't wanted to do it. Janey knew she'd felt embarrassed at such a public announcement that money was short.

She opened the door and a close, musty smell came to her. He walked past and went to the one window and raised it. She felt a sudden cross breeze that cleansed the air and ruffled her clothing. Then she smelled the sharp, masculine scent of gasoline or motor oil and knew it must have come from his hands. He turned and looked at her, and she grew uncomfortable again under his gaze, though she didn't feel as if he were looking at her as a woman, the way a woman might want if it was the right man. She felt she'd gone past the age for that and into a settled middle age. It was a passing she'd mourned, then gotten over.

He lifted his hand slowly and held it in front of his chest. His palm was stained with what looked like motor oil. She couldn't have been more surprised at the sight of his fingers moving. "I like the room," he spelled out. "I'll take it."

That was all. No conversation, no explanation about when or why he'd learned to speak, or how he'd known for certain that she was deaf. But his large fingers had moved quickly and easily.

He walked past her again, and this time she followed him. He spoke briefly to her mother, then went down the porch steps and away, his movements purposeful, businesslike.

"He's going to get his car from where he left it at the store," her mother said.

She started to tell her mother how he had spoken, then decided not to, at least for now. It would be some small thing she could keep to herself, or maybe for herself.

Only two other people in Riverfield had ever known how to speak to her, an Episcopal minister who'd finally moved to a larger church in Selma, and Louise Anderson, whose son owned the store where the man was now headed. Louise had learned as an offer of friendship, and when she visited, the two of them sitting out on the porch, their hands flying with words and sometimes a little gossip, her mother would stand in the dark of the doorway, watching, and would finally emerge and tell Janey that she needed her for some chore, usually one that had either already been done or didn't need doing. She'd always been this way, continually calling Janey to her, but after Janey's father had died, it had grown worse.

Janey signed a question for her mother now.

"He works for the WPA," she said, again speaking too slowly. "Travels around the state taking pictures."

"Of what?"

"Buildings. Old houses and slave quarters, plantation homes. Says there are people like him doing this all over the South."

"Our house?" Janey said.

Her mother nodded and looked down. She knew why. The house wasn't what it had been. The roof needed replacing. The steps were warped. Her grandfather, Jason Teclaw, had built the house with slave labor, and made a large, comfortable home, the one oddity in its design the columns across the front and side of the house. The branch stubs at the tops of the tree trunks they'd used had never been completely cut away, so each column looked as though it grew up out of the ground. There were knotholes, too, visible in the sides of each column, and now that the paint on the house was completely gone, the columns looked even more like trees that had reached a certain height and had their growth stunted or stopped. Bricks around the cellar walls had come loose, leaving holes into the darkness that had once been, for a brief period, the saloon that had gotten her grandfather kicked out of the Methodist congregation. He'd then bought the Episcopal church that stood in the next county, had it dismantled and shipped across the Tennahpush River, and finally erected where it stood now, just down the road from where Janey had heard her last sound.

Music was her entry into silence. She'd been only ten years old, sitting on the end of the porch above the steps, listening to the Episcopal choir rehearse "Our God to Whom We Turn" not fifty yards away. Their voices had carried easily through the open church doors and on the light breeze, and that breeze had felt like music itself against her skin. Then her head began to reel and spin, and she fell backwards into sound and air and finally nothing as all her senses went dark.

She woke into darkness nights later, there in her room, in her bed. She'd called out from her confusion as any child would, and her mother was there instantly, always her mother. But something sounded wrong, or had not sounded, except inside her where illness and confusion grew. She hadn't heard herself, hadn't heard the call she'd made—*Mama*. And though her mother was already gripping her tightly, she'd called out again, but only into silence, which is where she lived now, had been living for so many years that she didn't feel uncomfortable inside its invisibility. Sometimes she thought it saved her, gave her a separate place to retreat into as far as she might need at any given moment—and there were moments.

After he had unloaded his car and carried in his suitcase and camera and other equipment, Mr. Clark asked her about meals. "He wants room and board," she told her mother, who was pleased at the chance to bring in a little more money.

He ate a supper of soup and cornbread with them that night, at the table in the middle of the kitchen. They'd had plenty of soup left from the day before, and Janey had made the cornbread herself, though it was never as good as her mother's, which her mother always found ways to point out.

"Nice to have good cooking," Mr. Clark said, but he wouldn't respond to the protests pointed at him by her mother about how poor the soup tasted. He appeared indifferent at the hints for another compliment. He mostly remained silent, nodding when he had to, watching first her mother, then her, studying them, it seemed, from some far-removed place, where quiet held value.

But the quiet soon became more than her mother could bear. "Are you married, Mr. Clark?" she said. She spoke quickly, abruptly. Janey wondered if her mother hadn't wanted her to read the question, but she'd seen the shape of the words. She'd also noticed earlier that he didn't wear a wedding ring, just as her mother must have noticed.

He nodded *yes*, but offered nothing else, not even his wife's name.

Then her mother must have asked another question, but her face had been turned away.

"She's staying with her folks now, in Calera, while I travel," he said.

"Children?" she spoke quickly again, but Janey had seen.

"No," he said and looked down, as though children had been something denied him.

Her mother's expression turned suddenly sad. "I don't know what I'd do without my daughter beside me," she said, and Janey looked then at Mr. Clark, and his eyes shifted back and forth between them. Finally he looked away, as though he'd taken some partial measure of them, or perhaps she'd only imagined it.

In the morning he loaded his camera and tripod into his car. He'd told her mother at breakfast, when she asked, that he'd begin with some of the buildings clustered around the post office and the store. It was a short walk, but he couldn't have carried everything he needed, so loading the car was a necessity.

He had hardly acknowledged Janey at breakfast, but now, after closing the car door, he walked toward where she sat. She tensed at his approach, perhaps because of his own tense expression. He looked tired, irritated. Maybe her mother had said something to him, or asked one too many questions.

"You might be able to help me," he signed.

She'd half expected him to say he'd be leaving by the end of the day, and felt more relief at his asking her for help than she would have anticipated. Afraid of him or not, she liked what his presence made her feel. "If I can," she spelled with her fingers.

"I'll need to know something about the buildings, the ones I take pictures of, for my notes. Maybe tonight you can tell me some history about them, who built them."

"I'd be glad to try. I can certainly tell you about this house."

She watched him back out of the drive, and felt glad to be needed, useful in some small way. When she stood to go inside, she caught her mother watching from the door.

"You didn't tell me," her mother said.

"What?"

"You know."

"That he knows how to speak to me?"

"Yes, that."

"No, I didn't tell you," she said, suddenly bold, thrusting her hand as she formed the letters and made her irritation clear.

Her mother turned and walked into the house. Janey felt her footsteps in the boards of the porch. The floor had always carried her mother's anger. She'd learned this first as a little girl when her mother and father argued. Their words might not have existed as sound for her, but anger always caused its own vibration.

She hadn't been exactly sure why they argued all those years ago, but sensed, the way a child will, that it was usually about her. And when she grew older she decided that it must have been about what she could and couldn't do, about what would be allowed and what wouldn't, and finally about what would be done with her, or for her, though she couldn't have put all of this into words as a child, words thought or spoken—in any form.

After their arguments her mother would come to her, take her into the kitchen while she worked, keeping her close, the stove's heat encircling her, pressing against her, taking her breath almost with its expansion through the room. Then her father might come in later, pick her up or take her by the hand, and quickly they would go out of the house and up to the store or maybe to the depot to watch the afternoon train arrive and depart northward. He would sit with her, hold her hand, smoke his cigar, the smell and smoke surrounding them in a masculine world of men loading and unloading, of coal and iron rails and more smoke and dreams of departure, the two of them headed away.

And then they did head away, but not before more silences and anger that she felt kept her parents from listening to each other, each made deaf in his or her own way. But the day arrived when, her suitcases packed, she and her father boarded the train for Talladega. After three days, he left her there, settled, as best she could be at the age of twelve, in her dorm room and in a school for the deaf and blind.

She'd loved it there, had learned the alphabet on her fingers and how to sign, and how to read lips. She'd continued, finally, with her regular schooling too, and taken art and began to paint with oils. The other children there were like her, lived in her world of silence that was no longer quiet but filled with the voices of fingers and hands flying—thin fingers, long fingers, the beautiful hands of boys. It was wonderful to be able to give shape to words. She knew that her speaking voice was something she'd had less and less control over, and so seldom used it. Now words came through her fingers, the muscles there growing stronger and more sure, giving her a voice again, a voice that wanted to shout, or even sing.

Her mother wouldn't visit, but wrote desperate letters about home, about missing her and wanting her there, those cursive words on the page like pieces of string tying and knotting her emotions. During her trips home she taught her father to speak to her, but for the longest time her mother could not, or would not, learn. "You can read lips," she would say. "That's enough for me."

"What about me?" she'd sign, and, of course, no answer came, and wouldn't have even if she'd forced herself to ask it aloud, from out of her throat and off her tongue.

Her mother wouldn't want her to go places with her father, would become silent and withdrawn when they returned. She didn't want Janey going to the store by herself, even for a quick errand. One day her mother found her playing in the woods behind their house, and when she wouldn't follow her mother home, her mother grabbed her by the arm and yanked her through the trees. She finally yanked back and shouted at her, not in words but in her old voice that expressed all she felt in one great vibration. Her mother spoke with a hand then. She slapped her hard across her face.

When she left for school a week later, her mother wouldn't go with them to the depot but held her at the door. She felt her mother shaking and knew her mother loved her, but love was sometimes like silence, beautiful but hard to bear. At the train station her father told her, "She can't help herself. I don't know why. I never have."

Late that morning, from her place on the porch, she watched Mr. Clark work around the buildings in town. He moved his camera from one position to another, then disappeared beneath the black cloth before moving again. At intervals he'd go inside the store or speak to people passing. She'd thought he would come home for lunch, but he must have eaten at the store, perhaps asking questions for his notes. Maybe he wouldn't need her after all.

That afternoon she saw him load his car and expected him to soon pull into their drive, but watched with surprise, and disappointment, as he drove directly past, picking up speed and raising dust behind him. She spotted Uncle Silas, the old black man who'd worked for her father's side of the family, in the back seat and knew then where they were headed, several miles away to the old home of her father's people, her cousins, some of them several times removed. The house stood three stories with a cupola and had white columns and a grand porch, with slave quarters behind. He'd want pictures of all that, of course. Her mother wouldn't have wanted her to go up there with them. There was a distance between her mother and her father's people. It had always been there.

Her mother was bathing when he finally drove in. She'd been put out that he hadn't come at the time she'd told him supper would be ready.

"Tardiness is rude," she had said.

Janey waited, gave him time to put his things away, then went and tapped on his door, and as her knuckles hit against the wood, she felt that the door was closed on some secret, something private and obscure that she shouldn't approach.

The door opened suddenly, and he stood there with a small towel in one hand. She'd filled the washbasin on his dresser with fresh water earlier. He looked tired, but not angry or irritated.

"Supper's ready for you," she signed.

He nodded and followed her.

Once they reached the kitchen she fixed his plate and set it before him. He looked at her and motioned to the chair across the table. She hadn't known if she should sit with him or not and felt relief at his invitation.

He only ate at first and didn't try to speak, his hands being occupied. She sat and waited, watched him bent over his plate. Each movement he made was so deliberate and sure. His masculine demeanor seemed to make the whole house feel different, as if the house had a slightly altered design. He stopped eating finally and put his knife and fork down.

"People at the store told me what I needed for my notes. Others too. Everyone was curious and wanted to talk. It's like that everywhere."

She was certain that he saw her disappointment, no matter how hard she tried to hide it. He apologized then for being late, and it was as though he felt a need to say something considerate to assuage her feelings. He went on and told her, too, after taking a few bites, about driving out to the antebellum home of her father's side of the family, being polite enough not to mention the disrepair it was in. "Someone in town told me about the house," he was saying, and she saw that he'd begun to speak aloud as he signed—his lips were forming words—and she felt confused, couldn't understand why he would do this. She couldn't read his lips and watch him sign at the same time. He must have known that. He paused and studied her, watched her expression more closely. "I could have asked you to ride out there with me, couldn't I? You might have wanted to go. You might have enjoyed that. Some time away from here." He motioned around the room.

She looked toward the kitchen door, not aware at first why she turned that way. Perhaps she'd simply turned away from him out of embarrassment, or perhaps she understood, on some unconscious level, what she hadn't a moment before. Her mother was standing there. She'd been listening to him. He had wanted her to hear.

When she turned back to him she read his lips. "Why don't you go with me tomorrow?"

She felt the quick vibration of her mother's approach but wouldn't turn to face her. "Yes, ma'am," he was saying, looking past Janey. "I know, but she could help me. Be a guide. I could even pay her a little. Why don't we ask her?"

Janey saw his hard gaze still focused on her mother, maybe even gathered strength from it, and she stood then, turned to her mother, and saw her mother's anger and fear. She drew in her breath and forced the two breath-filled words out in a hoarse whisper that might have sounded, for all she knew, like a sick child or someone dying.

"I'll go," she said.

Her mother stared at her in surprise, and Janey wasn't sure if her mother was more shocked that she had used what was left of her voice, or at what she'd said. Mr. Clark showed no reaction at all but took another bite of food and drank from his glass.

"You can't. You just can't," her mother said. "I need you to help me with some things around the house tomorrow."

"No," she signed, then shook her head. "You don't."

"You know good and well I do. There's cleaning to be done."

"It will wait," she said and walked out before her mother could.

She went to her room and imagined the two of them at the table still, imagined what they might be saying, and her father came to mind suddenly. It was as if Mr. Clark had become, for the moment, the man her father had been, the two of them in there now acting out the old ritual of her parents, except this time she had spoken, and they both had heard her wishes.

She could still hear her father's voice, the memory of it clear in a way that her mother's wasn't. It had been deep, but not extraordinarily so, and gentle, though when he scolded her there was a sharpness to it that crushed her and made her want forgiveness, which always came quickly, and he would hold her and wipe her tears and smile.

It was the telegram that took him away from her, the one her mother sent and that she received at school. "Come home," it said. "Your father has died of fever." She was fifteen, and even then, after the first shock, she realized that the demand to come home had come first, as if coming home were more important than the death of her father. So she went, and saw her father buried, suffered the quiet of the funeral that she could not hear but only feel. A few days later she walked to the grave alone and left her handprints in the mound of dirt over his casket and body.

She stayed then, not quite strong enough without him to get back on the train, though she planned to and spoke of it as if she would, her mother ignoring her.

Two months later the school shipped her belongings home. The first she knew of it was when they were delivered from the depot in the back of a wagon. She saw the boxes and felt somehow that her life had been returned to her mother. Each box bore her mother's name.

Janey didn't see her the next morning, and she didn't look in her room to check on her, which is what she knew her mother wanted. Instead she bathed and dressed early, then fixed breakfast and packed a lunch for herself and Mr. Clark, putting everything away afterward, leaving no plate of food covered with a cloth.

She planned to take him up the road to Oakhill, show him the old house at the top of the hill, and introduce him to the people there. If she'd given him directions he could have found it on his own, but that didn't matter. He'd asked her to go with him, and he'd known what he'd really been asking. She'd entered into the conspiracy with him and needed to see it through. Not to would have been a kind of failure.

After he loaded the car she climbed into the passenger seat. When he stopped and filled up with gas at the store, she saw people looking at her in the car and enjoyed their curiosity. He drove too fast, and she felt an exhilaration at their increasing speed and at the plume of dust they raised that blocked her view of everything behind them. Neither tried to speak, and she had the feeling that even if his hands hadn't been busy, he would have remained quiet. The look on his face in profile was hard set, concentrated on something beyond driving it seemed.

The road rose toward Oakhill and at the top, before they turned into the long drive that led to the house, she saw the open pastures and fields spread out before her like a patchwork quilt and suddenly felt like a child wanting to run across them, as if they lay there waiting for her. A silly notion, but it made her smile.

The house stood beyond the oak grove and came into full view after they rounded a final curve. It was two-story with small white columns. No mansion, but clearly built by a land-owning family.

They got out of the car and walked up the steps to the porch. Janey knocked on the screen door and waited for Mrs. Spence to come, but instead an older black woman Janey knew as Aunt Minnie appeared in the hall and opened the door. She nodded at Janey and said, "How you, Miss Janey?" Then looked at the strange man beside her. "I bet you that picture man. I done heard about you."

Mr. Clark spoke, but Janey didn't catch any of his words.

"The mister and missus, they done gone into town, up to Valhia. Is you come to take pictures?"

Janey watched him speak this time. He asked if he could at least take pictures of the outside of the house since the owners weren't home.

She nodded. "They won't mind that, I don't reckon. What about my house, out back? You gon' take a picture of it? You can go inside. It's mine. Least I calls it mine." She smiled. "I'd like a picture took of it."

"I was going to ask you if I could," he said. "Inside too."

Janey wondered if he was speaking the truth or humoring her.

"Come on around," the woman said. "You can do the big house later."

They followed. Mr. Clark carried only a small camera around his neck. The large camera with the tripod and black cloth he left in the car for now.

Several outbuildings stood directly behind the house. One of them, Janey imagined, had been a kitchen back when they were built separately so heat wouldn't overtake the house in summer and, in case of fire, wouldn't burn down the entire home. Farther on stood a small, unpainted shack, one window to the right of the door. It had already occurred to her that she had never been in a black person's house, or in the house of someone so poor. She knew her mother hadn't either, just as her mother had never let those lost men traveling through come to the back door and eat a meal. Janey realized that if her mother had been with them that she would never set foot inside where they were headed, would be appalled at the idea, and wouldn't let Janey inside, not without protest and argument.

"My grandmother was born a slave in this house," the woman said now. "We always worked for the Spences. Far back as I know of."

Mr. Clark stopped and took several pictures of the front of the house. "You don't mind if we go on in?" he said when he finished.

"I keeps my house clean always. Not ashamed of anything I got either."

They walked onto the small porch and boards gave under their feet. Aunt Minnie went in first, then Mr. Clark. Janey held back a moment, imagined again what her mother would say if she knew, then stepped through the doorway into the cramped slave house and felt, in some place within herself, as if she'd walked into one of those open fields she had seen from the car, was straying like some child running just ahead of her mother.

The house was clean, neat, the bed made with a colorful quilt across it. Newspaper pages that had not yet yellowed covered the walls, cut and pasted as carefully as any new store-bought wallpaper. A calendar from Anderson's store with May 23rd circled hung by the door. There was a back window, and she noticed how clean the panes were, how the light broke through them and opened the room, made it somehow larger, as if it brought the whole of outdoors inside. The small black stove was wiped down, and the few pots and pans hung in order on the wall behind it. Aunt Minnie had been right. There was nothing here to be ashamed of, nothing to look down upon. Janey wished this were a place she could stay and felt a sense of envy. Then she decided no—she felt a kind of admiration for Minnie.

Mr. Clark took pictures, including one of Minnie in a chair beside the bed. She wasn't smiling but seemed at ease with herself and everything around her.

Once they were back outside, Mr. Clark got his large camera and set it up for pictures of the main house. He moved every few minutes, capturing the house at different angles. When he finished he told Minnie that he'd come again and see about taking some pictures inside, if the people didn't mind.

"Come on. They be glad to see you," she said. Then she asked if she might have a copy of the picture he'd taken of her.

"I'll see to it," he said. "It'll be a while, but I'll send it."

In the car Janey asked if he'd ever taken pictures inside a house like Minnie's.

"No," he said, and didn't elaborate. "I need those people home when I go back," he added after a moment.

His whole demeanor had changed, and Janey felt that she'd been chastised, that it was somehow her fault that the Spences hadn't been home.

A question came to her, one that she had to ask, though she feared the answer. "Do people often ask for copies of the photographs you take?"

"All the time," he signed, then put the car into gear.

"Do you send them?"

He looked away, kept his eyes on the narrow drive, and both hands on the wheel.

They drove to several churches spread around the countryside, their conversation minimal. He took pictures both inside and out, working quickly and methodically, clearly knowing exactly what he wanted as soon as he saw each structure. They ate the lunch that she'd packed at a table on the grounds of a small A.M.E. church, and she didn't try to speak. He seemed even further removed, already traveling on his own. She wondered where he was in his mind, wondered if she had done something to make him more distant.

Late that afternoon he told her he wanted to head back, but had one more stop in mind, the Episcopal church near her house. When they parked in front of it she began to tell him how the church had been brought across the river and why. "Later," he signed. "Tell me later." Then he got out of the car.

She stood well away from him while he worked, wandered into the graveyard behind the church, and finally to her father's grave. The grass grew thick and neat over it, but she recalled the mound of bare dirt, the way it had felt against her hands when she placed them there, the way their prints looked so perfectly made, but so empty.

He appeared then, setting up his camera, and waited for her to move, without asking, so he could take a picture of the back of the church with the gravestones in the foreground.

She obliged him, went around the building and sat on the steps at the double side doors. In a little while he walked around from the front and approached her, without his camera. He was clearly ready to go. She didn't move but looked up at him, then began to speak. He didn't turn away now but watched, though impatiently, it seemed. She didn't care.

"The last sound I ever heard came from here, through these open doors. Choir voices, all joined together. They were beautiful. A final gift to me."

She placed her hands in her lap and remained still, not really looking to see if he reacted or not to what she'd said. He turned slowly and walked away, but she didn't follow. She could easily walk home by herself, decided she'd like to do just that, but not quite yet. She wanted to be alone.

He came back though, carrying the small camera around his neck. She looked up at him but kept still. He raised the camera slowly, peered through it, then lowered it after a moment and stepped toward her. He reached out with his right hand and touched her just under her chin. The warmth of his fingers made a dampness on her skin. He gently turned her face at a more downward angle, then backed away and adjusted the camera. She watched the shutter close and open and imagined the sound it made, imagined what part of her the camera might capture.

Her mother had been up while they were gone. Janey saw a book left open on the sofa, and there was a single dish left in the kitchen sink. She wondered if her mother had heard them pull into the drive and gone quickly to her room, not expecting them back quite so early. She was probably in bed, pretending to be asleep. Of course it was possible that she was sick. She did tire more easily these last few years. Still Janey wouldn't go to her, and if she didn't, she knew that her mother would finally show herself.

She did, before good dark came. Janey was sitting in a chair on the porch, by herself, considering what she might do about supper. Her mother walked out of her bedroom door, the one that opened directly onto the porch and that she seldom used. She sat down in the chair next to Janey.

"Have you not been feeling well today?" Janey knew what the answer would be.

Her mother shook her head, then looked away for a moment.

"Do you feel like you can eat something?"

"Whatever you can fix," she said, then turned away again. It was something she did often, the turning away, a way of ignoring Janey, of not listening, because it took sight for her to be listened to. Sometimes it amused Janey, her mother's turning, but not now. She had been ignored enough today. She thought about telling her mother where they'd gone, about going inside Aunt Minnie's house and taking pictures—just to see her reaction, for spite, she guessed. But she stayed quiet. Upsetting her mother would have been too easy, and maybe pointless.

She watched the evening come on, remembered the glissando of locusts at this time of year from when she was a little girl, and wondered if they were out there now, appearing from their years-long silence and making their one sound.

Her mother looked toward the front door and Janey saw Mr. Clark had walked out of his room. He'd changed into a fresh shirt and was rolling the sleeves up. He greeted her mother, then stood before them as if he had something important to say. This time Janey turned, perhaps afraid of what he might announce. He wouldn't be staying with them for months, or even weeks. How many more days would it be?

When she looked back at them she saw the words *colored churches* form on Mr. Clark's lips. Her mother's eyes widened. "You went inside them?"

"A few," he said, studying her, measuring her reaction. He looked at Janey then, as though he were waiting on her to speak, and when she didn't he continued, his eyes lingering on her, perhaps taking some measure of her this time. "The Spences weren't home, but we went in one of the shacks up at Oakhill. Aunt Minnie's house. An old slave quarters."

Her mother looked down at her feet, closed her eyes, and slowly shook her head, as if she'd received news that someone was ill. "You shouldn't be going into colored people's houses, Janey," she said. "At least the Spences weren't there to see you."

Mr. Clark seemed to be waiting on Janey again, and something inside her didn't want to disappoint him.

"Why not?" she said. "Why not go into a colored person's house?"

"You know why. Because it doesn't look good." She stood, seemed to have regained her strength, and walked back into her bedroom, clearly unwilling to respond to any more such absurd-sounding questions.

Mr. Clark nodded at Janey, which she understood as a kind of approval, but something about it bothered her, made her feel presided over, and the way he stood there, above her, made her uncomfortable, as she had felt with him early on. Before she realized what he was doing, he walked to the end of the porch, down the steps, and kept going, past his parked car—headed to the store, she imagined. She realized she would be eating alone that night.

Her mother remained secluded in the morning, which Janey had expected. What she hadn't been sure of was whether or not Mr. Clark wanted her to go along with him again, but at breakfast he made clear that he did. She told him about some of the larger houses down toward the Tennahpush River that he might want to look at. He seemed more open to listening to her today, his mood changed from the day before.

She made a lunch for them while he loaded his car. When she walked out the front door and pulled it to behind her, she suddenly expected to see her mother's door open, and it did. Her mother stood there in her bedclothes and without a robe, motioning to Janey, the door angled between herself and Mr. Clark at his car.

"What, Mother?" she signed.

"I don't feel well."

"I know that."

"I mean I'm worse today."

Janey took a few steps toward her and then looked past the oddly made columns surrounding the porch. Mr. Clark stood against the front of his car, his arms folded, watching her, waiting.

"My chest hurts," her mother said, "and my breath doesn't come easy. You know I don't have a normal heartbeat."

Janey knew about the irregular heart, and had heard all these complaints before, too many times to take them seriously.

"Come here," her mother said, and held out a piece of paper. "Please, I've got to get back in bed."

Janey walked to her and took the paper. It was a note to Dr. Hannah asking him to come see her.

"There's nothing wrong with you," she said. "We both know that."

"You can't go with that man today. I need you here," she said aloud. "I need you to bring the doctor here." For once she wasn't speaking slowly.

Janey looked and saw Mr. Clark at the bottom of the steps now, waiting, impatient, wanting what he wanted from her. Her mother pulled the door closer to her, but didn't retreat back into the room, though she seemed to sense Mr. Clark's nearness.

She wanted to retreat, to surrender into the most silent of places within herself, where her own thoughts couldn't find voice.

"All right," she said finally. "I'll stay and get the doctor just to prove to you there's nothing wrong, and that's the only reason. I'll go with him tomorrow."

Her mother nodded, clearly relieved, and slowly shut the door.

Janey walked down to Mr. Clark. He hadn't moved. His expression said nothing.

"I can't go today," she signed. "I've got to get the doctor. Tomorrow I'll go."

"There's nothing wrong with her." He signed the words.

"I know."

"Then get in the car. Now."

"I can't."

He focused his eyes on her the way he might when he looked through a camera, capturing her, exposing her weakness for her to see. His face showed neither pity nor disgust. Whatever was there she couldn't read the way she could spoken words, and he didn't give her any further opportunity. He turned, climbed inside his car, and drove away, leaving her standing alone in the middle of the drive. She pulled her mother's note from her pocket, held it in her hand, and felt for a moment as if it were meant for her, like one of her mother's letters that came for her when she'd been at school.

Doctor Hannah walked out of her mother's room, his black bag in his hand. He looked tired already, even at mid-morning. He began to speak carefully, and quietly, she knew, so that her mother couldn't overhear. "There's nothing wrong, other than maybe nerves."

"Her heart?" Janey wrote on a small notepad.

"She's had an arrhythmia since I first came here and saw her as a patient, but there's been no deterioration. I'm certain of that. My only mistake was telling her about it."

"So she's fine?"

He nodded. "I gave her a shot, a mild sedative, to calm her nerves. That's all."

"Thank you," she wrote.

He smiled slightly and touched her shoulder for a moment, the way her father might have. She imagined that going into people's homes and seeing to the ill had taught him a lot about what people needed, both the sick and the well.

She checked on her mother after lunch and found her sitting up in bed.

"I'm feeling better now. I knew seeing Dr. Hannah would help."

Janey didn't respond, didn't move past the door's threshold.

"I'm going to bathe and dress," her mother said. "Could you fix me something to eat? I'll take it in my room so I won't tire myself out."

She slowly signed yes, glad for the moment that she no longer used speech, because she knew how angry her tone would have sounded. But what would that have mattered? Except for the fact that she was most angry at herself. For staying. She should have been in the car with Mr. Clark. He wouldn't be here much longer, and after he was gone nothing would be changed. Perhaps that was what made her most angry. His presence had shown her something that she'd kept her eyes closed to—a willful blindness on her part, another killing of the senses.

She finally carried a tray to her mother and saw that she'd dressed and put on makeup.

"This is so nice. Thank you," her mother said slowly.

Janey only nodded.

She wasn't aware that Mr. Clark had returned until she looked out a front window and happened to see his camera set up in the yard. She didn't see him, though, and then there he was, back at the camera, about to pull the dark cloth over his head. She tried to picture what he saw—the rusted roof, the unpainted boards, the strange columns with branches cut short, all of it upside down, and she felt as though everything inside herself had fallen out of place, all of it turned by his hand.

He moved the camera from one place to another, and she watched from various windows, careful to stand far enough away so that her image wasn't captured behind a pane.

When she saw him photographing the back of the house, she walked onto the porch and waited for him to come back around front. She wondered if he would take pictures inside too. Sometimes he did, sometimes not.

It surprised her when she saw him at his car in the drive, bent over beside it, but there he was, loading his equipment again. He was going back out. She could go with him now that she had seen to her mother. Perhaps that was why he'd come, not just to take the pictures but to give her another opportunity. She stood when he finished loading, ready to leave without a word to her mother, and he turned and saw her. She expected him to motion to her, or to speak with his hands, but after the briefest glance her way, he opened the driver's side door and climbed in, his face shadowed by the brim of his hat, and then all of him disappeared behind the glare of the sun on the windshield.

His coming in the middle of the afternoon must have been only one more stop for him, one more house to photograph and move away from. But he had to have come when he did for a reason. It would have made so much more sense for him to take pictures of her house as his last stop of the day. Maybe he had been taunting her, or speaking his anger at her as loudly as he knew how—treating her as no more important than a stranger at yet another stop.

He backed all the way to the road, and though there were no cars coming from either direction, he sat idling. Moments passed. She was puzzled, and couldn't see if he was looking her way or not. She remained still, waiting, for what she didn't know. Maybe he was waiting too, giving her one more chance to come down the steps on her own. Then he was gone.

It was well past dark, late, in fact, after eleven o'clock, when he returned. She felt his steps through the house, felt his door closing. She looked out her front window to see if he would make the trips to unload his car, which was something he never failed to do, but he didn't come back out. Maybe he'd driven all the way to town, to Demarville, for a meal at the hotel, and then found a drink some-where. Or maybe he'd found a drink here and had never gone into town at all or bothered with supper.

She didn't sleep. At eleven-thirty she sat up in bed and pulled on her robe. She stood then, telling herself she was going into the kitchen, but when she found it empty, as she knew she would, she walked slowly and softly to the front door, opened it, and stepped into the house's entryway. The distance he had shown her the last two days drew her to his door, and emboldened now in the way she should have been earlier in the day, she knocked twice.

He opened the door after a moment. A lamp was burning, and she saw he was still dressed in shirt and pants. She also smelled liquor, strongly, but he appeared in control of himself, though he looked disheveled, his shirttail out, his sleeves rolled up loosely, not into his usual neat cuffs, though revealing again his strong forearms. He motioned for her to sit in the one chair, and he sat on a chest at the foot of the bed. He didn't seem surprised to see her, which she found unsettling.

She started to tell him that she'd wanted to leave with him after he'd taken pictures of her house, but she decided he already knew that. There was no need to say it.

"If you'd just waited another minute," she signed, knowing he'd understand.

Except for a barely perceptible nod, if only to let her know that he was reading her, he didn't respond.

His silence was as frustrating as before. She needed him to talk. He already knew what she had to say. Did he have anything at all to say to her?

He looked at her through squinted, shadowed eyes. "I knew about you before I came," he signed.

"How?" she said. "What did you know?"

"That a deaf woman and her mother lived here, that they sometimes rented a room. In one town, I ask about the next, or what might be the next. So I heard that, and came."

"Why?" she asked, uncertain if he would say more.

He remained still at first, his hands at rest. Then he looked at her, studied her. "I was told there were places here I ought to take pictures of. This place too, the columns with the limbs on them. I wanted to see that, to make a record of it."

She waited again, for what he hadn't said yet. She saw that she would have to push him. "The deaf woman you heard about—I'm part of why you came."

He nodded, but that was all.

"Why?"

"My mother," he said, as though she could follow.

The lamp grew dimmer and the shift in light seemed to carry him further away from her.

"My mother lost her hearing when I was very young. She was still young too, but I didn't know how young, not then. I learned to sign as she learned." He paused, then his hands seemed to find the words in the air. "My father didn't."

"What?"

"Didn't learn. Didn't treat her well. He never had."

She became bold again, understanding through some instinct she didn't know she had, then spelling it out. "He hit her."

He nodded again, slowly, even further away from her now, carried away by memory, and perhaps more alcohol than she'd realized.

"She suffered. It was terrible. There were awful beatings, and more and more of them."

She saw the anger in him still, in his face and clenched fists. It had been there all along, when he'd first walked to the porch with her mother, but it had taken this long to recognize it, and words from him to understand it.

"What happened?" She asked the question with a building fear, not of him but of what the answer might be.

"She took me. We left in the night."

She sighed with relief, but another question came to her. "She's dead now?" She felt she knew the answer.

"Yes." His hands stopped a moment, hung in the air. "It didn't take him long. He found her."

She took the words from his hands, felt the weight of them within her. "And you?" she managed to ask.

He shrugged his shoulders. He was through—or almost.

"Your wife?" she said then, trying to imagine the life he might have made for himself, already fearing the answer.

"There's no wife. There never has been."

She simply nodded.

"My mother tried. She did what she could, for me and for herself. I owe her a debt for that, and have to find someone to pay."

Even in the dim room she saw the brightness in his eyes, their focus directly on her, and she became afraid, of him this time, and of what she caught glimpses of behind the reflection of light in his eyes. She felt she saw ghosts within him, his mother's and his own ghost, small and lost.

She awoke knowing that he was gone. When she rose and checked his room, she found the door open, the bed made, and none of his belongings. He'd left the window open too for some reason. She felt the cross breeze.

Within an hour she'd dressed and tried to occupy herself with cleaning, but her work was careless, and she knew it. She finally put the dusting cloth away and gave in to a sense of mourning for something lost.

Her mother hadn't gotten up by noon. Perhaps this was her way of making Janey check on her. It wouldn't work, not this time. But after an hour passed, she entered the room and saw her mother was awake but still in bed and wouldn't rise from her pillow. Janey walked closer and started to sign, but she saw the stare then and knew, saw the lack of any movement, not even the gentle lifting and falling of the sheet across her body.

She felt a greater loss to mourn now, and it fell upon her heavily, in a way she might not have expected. She sat at the foot of the bed, looked again at her mother's stare, and wondered if she had known death was coming. Had it come from inside her, out of the irregular beat of her heart, or had she seen it walk into the room and bend over her, its hands reaching for the pillow on which she now lay? She felt she knew the answer, but knew she would not speak it, would say only that her mother had been up after Mr. Clark left, if anyone wanted to ask. If no one did, her silence would speak for her, as it always had.

HAINTS AT NOON

Field Notes: Federal Writers' Project (FWP) interview, Lottie Eppes, 97. Riverfield, Ala. September 12, 1936.

THESE BE HARD TIMES, SURE 'NOUGH, but they ain't hard like what us had before Freedom come. I was born on the Teclaw Place, and ain't far from it now as the crow fly. Ain't never been far from it in all my days.

Marster Will wasn't no good marster, but I heard tell a worse. Us didn't starve, but us got hungry some. Three pounds a meat, a peck of meal, and potatoes every week 'bout all we got. A little fatback and syrup. Maybe a chicken on Sunday if us picked enough cotton.

Most old folks like me, they tell some, but they ain't gon' tell all what could be tole, just what white folks wants to hear. In these hard times now, black folks needs what they can get from white folks and be scared somebody gon' take it away. Me, my day soon to come. I ain't got no worry 'bout nothin'. What anybody gon' take from me?

So I tell what some won't.

They was plenty whippings. Marster had a pole out past us Quarters, by the nigger box. If you wasn't whipped, it was the box they put you in. All you could do was stand up, just enough room to turn 'round inside. They was some air holes so you could suck in a little breath out the heat. Cornbread made without salt, and some water, was all you got, and not much a neither. Some stayed in long as a couple months. Me, a week, twiced, for stealing a biscuit and for not picking enough cotton when I's sick.

But them whippings was worse. I seed plenty of 'em. Never did get no whippings myself. Not like I's talking 'bout. Just the one, the one what brought out the haints.

I jumped the broom when I's fifteen, me and Isaiah. He was a few years older than me, but come up on the Teclaw Place and always showed me his attentions. So it felt right and natural for us to marry up. Us had two childr'n, boy and a girl. Ella, I don't know where she be now. Lord, I pray she live and well. My boy, Joshua, he send me letters from Memphis what the postmistress read for me. I right proud he learned his letters. He got childr'n too, and grandchildr'n. I ain't never seed 'em.

Not long before the war, Isaiah started to take him a notion. I didn't know what it be at first. All I knowed was he real quiet at night, hardly pay me no mind, or the childr'n neither. I thought he sick, maybe sick in his mind, and he near 'bout was. One day he say, "They a cave I found 'bove the river." He mean the Tennahpush. "Big enough for a man to hide in, it look like." Then I knew what notion took hold a him.

I got so scared. "What you mean?" I say. He ain't never have talked like that in all his days. Sound like a stranger. He'd been dreaming too much, what it was. And dreaming never was no good thing for one a us back then.

So he say he got it all figured. We gon' save back some food, store it in the cave. Then he gon' hide in there, stay long enough till every-thing quiet down and the patterollers and Marster Will quit looking. After a few days, he gon' head up North. Travel at night. "What 'bout me? And the childr'n?" I say. He gon' send for us. That what he tell me. "How?" I wants to know. He say when he free, he gon' work and buy our freedom.

He'd done dreamed hisself out a his mind, and made me sick in mine.

He stole him some rope, and late one night, us went to the river. He tied the rope to a tree at the top a that high chalk bank and let hisself down to the hole what he'd seen. Then he put the food in and climb back up, sayin' it a little bigger inside than what he thought.

Some days and nights go by, and he don't say when he leavin'. "How you gon' make enough buy our freedom?" I tell him. "Marster Will ain't gon' sell anyway." He don't say nothin', just look way off.

Then it come. "This the night," he say. The childr'n was sleeping and he don't wake 'em up. We gets to the river, and he tell me not to cry. Tell me when he get down there and call back up, for me to untie the rope and hide it. He don't want no sign pointing where he hidin'. Say the hole low enough, he can jump in the river when it time and swim 'cross.

I watch him climb down, then hear him call out, knowing it the last time I ever hear his voice. The tears come. I couldn't a stopped 'em.

Sleep never come take me that night. I kept thinking 'bout the childr'n and what us gon' do without they daddy. Then a notion took hold a me, one what made my spirit shake and tremble inside, enough for it to 'bout turn loose. You got to remember, I's young still, and scared. I done what I thought I had to.

Marster Will didn't take no dogs. I watched all the white mens leave out, and thought, Lord, Isaiah gon' know. Didn't matter if I were with 'em or not. He'd see me standin' there on the riverbank even if I wasn't there.

When they come back with him, they went straight to the pole by the nigger box. Us all had to turn out, even the childr'n. He seen me, and then he wouldn't look my way no more. The overseer the one what done it, with Marster Will looking on. He used the long whip, the one with the nine loose braids they kept locked up 'long with the good saddles. Every time Isaiah hollered out, I hollered out with him like it me they whipping. Us made a terrible sound, like a racket not even the devil could hardly a stood.

After they cut him loose, he fell down the way a empty sack would a done. Then the mens carried him to the house. He couldn't talk, but he wouldn't of anyway. I knew he wouldn't have no words to say to me.

I made the childr'n stay outside and went to washing all them cuts. Was so many you couldn't count 'em. Look like a butcher done chopped him up. He moan some, and moan some more when I put the salve to him. The hollerin' didn't start back till the next day when I washed them blisters with saltwater.

He let me work on him, but he still wouldn't talk none, not a word. And wouldn't look at me neither. He ain't had never acted such a way. Always'd been good to me and the childr'n, gentle-like. But him not talking, seemed every word he didn't say make me feel worse and worse. Got to where I couldn't eat. Didn't want no food. Felt like I done been put in the box for a month and wouldn't never get out 'less I died. Thought 'bout going ahead on and gettin' myself throwed in that thing. Knew it wouldn't be hard.

But something else come to my mind. A little after dark, after me and the childr'n done ate, I snuck to the barn and reached off what hung on the peg beside a stall. I tipped back and sent the childr'n out, and when he come home I had that little old bullwhip laid out on top the table. When he seen it, that when he finally looked at me, steady-like, studyin' on me, like he ain't never have seen me before. He went to shaking his head real slow and closed his eyes. I didn't say one word but took my dress part way down and got on the floor on my hands and knees.

I waited and waited, ready for it, but he didn't move none. "This the way it got to be," I finally say. "Please," I's beggin' him, whispering low and moanin' from way down inside, down where my spirit done start to come loose. I's crying, "Please, Isaiah."

He stay still, but then I hear his footsteps. Five times he done it, and then dropped the whip from out his hand and he fell down to the floor hisself, all in a heap, like he dead. And I thought, Lord, what I done done? I never get out that nigger box now. It nailed shut on every side.

He wash them cuts and put the salve to me, but us don't talk none. I hurt too bad, and I reckon he did too. The childr'n come in, and they seed me cleaning blood from the leather and puttin' oil to it. They too scared to ask me no questions. Whole house stay quiet as midnight.

Next day was Sunday. Every step hurt, but I's walkin' to the well, trying to keep my arms still while I moved 'long with the water bucket. The sun was straight up, and I seed Isaiah standin' between the well and the barn. Look like he waitin' on somebody, but he don't look exactly right. Look mostly like a shadow of hisself. I almost call out, but I knowed he ain't left the house. That put my mind to wonderin'. Then a cloud pass over and everything a shade. That when I seed myself. I knowed it was me right off. My spirit had done turned all the way loose, and I watched who I was walk right on up to Isaiah. Us stood there a minute. Didn't look at me atall. Then us started to walk off into the field, and when the cloud pass away and the sun come again, us was gone.

MIDNIGHT SHIFT

HE DIDN'T REALLY KNOW HER, but here it was midnight and she stood in his kitchen, the phone to her ear and a hand on her large hip. "Thomas, you better get home quick," she said. "My water just broke."

If she'd said, "I'm about to have a two-headed baby," he couldn't have been more shocked. David suddenly imagined her flat on her back, her thick legs spread across his linoleum floor with him crouched between them waiting for a dark head to appear. Yeah, Thomas, he thought, get your ass home and get this crazy girl out of my apartment.

She hung up the phone and walked into the small living room. He took a good look at her stomach but because of the extra weight she carried he still could not see any sign of a child.

"Thanks," she said. "They ought to have our phone back on soon." She stood there then, chewing her gum.

He wasn't sure what to say, but it was pretty clear that she was waiting on him to say something. "You having labor pains?" he finally asked.

"No," she said. "Not yet anyway."

"There anything I can do? I could take you on to the hospital if you need." He prayed she would say no.

"Thomas is getting off work. He'll be home soon." Her face went blank for a moment, as if she had forgotten something important she was supposed to say. "He wants to take care of me, and the baby." She looked down at her feet and seemed to search for more words, but none came.

Just when he decided he would have to ask her to sit and wait, she began crying, not hard, but enough for the tears to show.

"I got to go. Thanks," she said and was out the door, onto the porch of the duplex, slamming her own door behind her. He didn't attempt to follow. He'd never had much luck following after a woman.

It was the longest conversation they'd ever had. Usually they only passed on the porch steps and barely spoke, though he didn't think he had ever been downright rude to her. The only other thing he knew about her was her name, Georgine. And that her black hair looked too dark for her somehow.

He wasn't even sure exactly how long she'd lived next door. Thomas had moved in about a year before, and David hadn't minded having a black neighbor, as long as he was quiet, and Thomas was. Then the girl started coming and going. The only thing David had thought at the time was that with just the one, Thomas had more white girl-friends than he did. As best as he could tell, she'd moved in, then back out, and Thomas had taken to parking his truck behind the duplex in the backyard, often enough so the grass died underneath it. He'd kept his blinds shut too, and the television turned down low. David was pretty sure she lived there now, and figured the baby had brought them back together.

In a few minutes he heard Thomas's red, low-rider truck pull in. He looked through his bedroom window and saw Thomas sitting in the cab adjusting the rearview mirror while the truck idled. The sound of the engine grew louder a couple of times, and he knew Thomas was mashing the accelerator.

Georgine finally walked out. "You could of at least come inside and checked on me."

If Thomas answered her, David did not hear. The two of them slowly drove away.

Maybe he could get back to sleep now. Work would come early, and he had to take inventory. His ex-wife had always told him it was funny how he could manage an auto-parts store but was the worst mechanic she'd ever seen. The last time she had walked out the door, he'd followed her, but it hadn't done any good.

When he left for work in the morning, the red truck sat in the drive again. David wasn't sure what that meant. Maybe the proud new papa was catching up on some sleep before he went back to the hospital.

He came home for lunch, which he often did. This time the truck was gone and an old blue four-door sat in its place, a car he had never seen before. A white man, in his mid-fifties at least, stood on the porch, knocking on Thomas's door. It was an odd sight somehow. Maybe the man was a bill collector, or worked for the realty company that rented the duplex. He tried looking in the window, then came down the steps.

David walked past him in the drive, nodded, and when the man nodded back David saw such a tired, worn-out expression that for a moment he felt a little better about his own life. Neither of them spoke. The man seemed too preoccupied to make the effort.

It was only after he had walked into his apartment and closed the door that David realized who the fellow must be. He turned on his radio and took his shoes off, then heard a knock at his own door. He wondered what the man could want from him.

Edgar had known for a while now where his daughter lived, but he'd only been to the apartment one other time. No one had answered then, either. It wasn't the worst street in Demarville, and the fact that it came to a dead end maybe made it a little safer for her. He knew things had changed, but still, not everybody needed to ride by and see where a mixed couple lived. Just a few days before somebody had sent him two playing cards in the mail, cut in half and taped together—a king of spades and a queen of hearts. Probably from one of those punk boys who had made fun of her in high school, boys he'd wanted to strangle.

Almost two months had passed since he'd seen her, or spoken to her. She'd been the one who did the shouting that last time, calling him a racist. "You think I'm just a nigger-lover, don't you?" she said.

He didn't think he was that way. When he sold insurance to black people, he was always glad to have their business, and never ripped them off like one agent he could name. But Lord, he'd never imagined having one as family, his blood kin, who he'd have to call his grandchild and take places—to the park, even to church. He often wondered just how dark the baby's skin would be, and couldn't believe he had to think about such a thing. His family, all its future generations, would be black, shaded to a darker and darker hue. It did not seem possible.

He knocked on the neighbor's door, and the face he saw looked a little friendlier this time, or maybe what he saw was more curiosity than anything else. "My daughter," he said, "girl with dyed black hair who lives here—wondering if you've seen her." Now the face looked puzzled.

"Last night. She had it yet?"

"What do you mean? Tell me what happened."

He listened as the man explained.

"And so his truck was back here this morning?" he said.

"Yeah, they didn't call you or nothing?" The tone of the voice registered surprise, but maybe concern too, and his expression softened.

Edgar let the question pass. "But it's too early for it to come yet."

"Maybe she's had it premature."

Or a miscarriage, he thought, and then felt guilty for wishing it, but maybe not guilty enough. "Did she seem like she was all right?"

"She was crying some, but wasn't hurting. Really, she wasn't."

He couldn't get a handle on the man's attitude toward his daughter, but he felt some level of sympathy toward himself. "I guess I better get to the hospital, see what's happened," he said.

"If I see either one of them, you want me to tell them you come by?"

He thought a moment. "No," he said, not sure why. "I guess not."

The man nodded as if he understood something Edgar didn't.

They didn't tell him much at the hospital, only that she'd been admitted, then been released within two hours. She couldn't have had the baby, and if there'd been a miscarriage, wouldn't they have at least kept her for the night? It didn't make sense. Where was she, and was there a baby?

He used a pay phone in the hospital lobby and tried to call Georgine's mother. No answer. She was either at work, hung over, or maybe drunk, or any combination of the three. They'd been divorced for years now. Georgine rarely saw her. He had been the one to raise their daughter. Now she seemed to hate him as much as she did her mother. The new American family—he guessed he sure had one of those now.

Not certain what else to do, he drove back to the duplex, hoping she might have shown up. He remembered that very first time he'd gone there looking for her. She had been staying at home with him again, and never said if she'd left Thomas on her own or if he'd kicked her out. Then she had stayed gone all night, and he didn't see her for the better part of two days. He became so worried that he had to go look for her. He'd tried peeking in a window after no one answered the door, but all the blinds had been closed. Something had made him walk around behind the duplex, and he'd seen the red truck sitting there. The coward, he thought, and had it confirmed when he went back to the door and knocked louder. He didn't think his daughter was there, just Thomas, hiding. Georgine came home that night and never said where she had been.

When he pulled into the shared drive, he saw the neighbor getting into his car. He stopped right behind him and the neighbor got out again and stood waiting. He didn't look irritated, only resigned.

"She's not at the hospital," he said and repeated what they'd told him at admitting.

"Kind of strange. Guess you don't know if you got a grandbaby or not."

"No, I don't. I take it they hadn't come by while I was gone."

"Not that I saw." He paused a moment, seemed to measure what he was about to say, as if there might be some risk involved in it. "Must be pretty tough on you."

Edgar knew by the way the man looked at him that he meant more than not being able to find Georgine. "A little, maybe," he said quietly.

The man slowly nodded. They both did, an almost imperceptible echo of movement.

"Can I ask your name?" Edgar said.

"It's David. Last name's Turner. I run the auto-parts store."

"You live here alone?"

"Since my wife and I split. I had to move somewhere."

"Sorry," he said. "Didn't mean to get personal. Must be tough."

David shrugged his shoulders. "I best get on back to work."

"I need to ask you a favor." He took out his wallet and tried to hand him a business card. "When you see her, can you call me? Maybe keep an eye on her and let me know what's going on?"

"I don't know if I ought to get involved with this. It's not like I really know her, or talk to her ever."

"She's my only child. She didn't even call me from the hospital. Please, I don't know what else to do."

"Just talk to her, man. That's what I'd do."

"You must not have children. It's not always that simple." He held out the card again.

David waved the card away as if it were a ticket to some place he didn't want to go. "Look, all I want is to work, come home, drink a beer, and mind my own business."

"Me too," he said. "That's the way I been living a long time, or trying to." He reached into his wallet again. "Just let me know if she's had the baby. Just that much. And take this for your trouble." He held out a fifty-dollar bill, and the card.

David closed his eyes, opened them, and looked at the ground. He finally took the card between his fingers.

"Look, you got an ex-wife, you've living in a tiny duplex, and your car's got too many miles on it. I know you could use the fifty. Take it. It's all right."

He drove back to his office, and by the time Edgar sat down at his desk, he felt bad about the offer he'd made but didn't want to think too much about what it was exactly that the two of them had bought and sold.

✳

When they left the hospital, Thomas had taken her to his sister's house, then gone back to work. Georgine told him she had wanted to go home, but he knew she needed sleep, and not on a urine-soaked mattress.

The doctor had explained. First he'd said the baby was fine, and the amniotic sack hadn't broken. Then he talked about pressure from the baby's weight, how it could empty the bladder. Once she heard, Georgine wouldn't look at him, or the doctor.

In the truck, facing her window, she said, "I can't believe I peed all over the damn bed." He knew he was supposed to say it was all right, but he couldn't. All he could think about was having to buy a new mattress, if she'd pissed as much as he was afraid she had. Still, he hadn't gotten mad at her or cussed any. That was something he ought to get credit for. And didn't he deserve credit for taking her back when she told him she was pregnant? Some wouldn't have. Friends told him she probably got pregnant on purpose, and that if he'd wanted a white girl he could have sure found a better one. It wasn't about her being white he'd told them. The two friends had just looked at each other.

He'd asked her once about getting pregnant on purpose. She had cussed him out, then cried. She could go from mad to sad quicker than any woman he'd ever seen, and take him right along with her. He felt like his life now was just like his truck, one low ride.

When his shift at the cement plant ended and he'd shoveled as much slag as he could stand, he went home and checked the mattress. The pad on top had caught most of it. He yanked off the covers and stood the mattress against the wall. After it aired out, he'd flip it over and put it back on the bed.

He took the pad and sheets to the laundromat and got them started washing. Then he drove to his sister's where he found Georgine still asleep. When she woke up, she started in again about their buying a crib. "All right," he said, wanting to say something to make her feel better, or maybe just to make her easier to be around. "Our baby sure got to have something to sleep on." At first she looked shocked. Then she smiled at him in a way he hadn't seen in a long time. He had told her once that when she smiled it was like the sun breaking through some dark clouds. He knew those clouds came from her not liking herself. It didn't take a genius to know that.

By the time they got home with the crib and clean sheets and pad, it was early afternoon. He fixed the bed, then slept.

When the doorbell rang, he wondered what time it was. He knew he'd been asleep a good while, but not nearly long enough. Then it rang again. Where in the world was she? He pulled some pants on and went to the door. David stood there with his hands in his pockets like he was trying to keep something hidden in them.

"You a daddy yet?"

"No, man," he said, then told him what had happened.

"Her old man came by looking for her around lunchtime."

"For real?" he said.

"I talked to him. He went to the hospital and came back. He doesn't know if she's had it yet or not." David tried to look past him into the apartment. "Georgine here?" he said in a low voice.

"I don't know where she's at, but wherever it is, she must a walked."

"Her daddy wants me to call him, let him know what's going on."

Thomas wasn't sure what to think about that. All he knew for sure was that her father didn't like him, or his skin color. "So you going to call him?"

"Think I should?"

"I know I ain't," he said.

"What about Georgine? You could tell her he came by looking for her, that he went to the hospital. Maybe she'd decide she wanted to call him."

"Maybe so. I'll have to think about it."

"He's plenty worried. If it was me, I'd call."

Thomas heard something in the tone of voice he didn't like. "You call him if you want. It don't make any difference. Guess I'd want to know something if I was him."

David looked at him and smiled. "You will be him one day."

"How's that?"

"A man worried about his kid, maybe a daughter."

"Won't be like that white man." He shook his head and slowly closed the door.

Thomas had met her father just one time, after he and Georgine had already broken up once or twice but before the baby. He had picked her up at her house and she'd pushed for him to come inside, said her daddy wanted to met him. Didn't much seem like it when he held his hand out to the man, but her father finally looked at him and offered his own. It was cold and wet from the bottle of beer he'd been drinking.

"Good to meet you," Thomas had said.

Her father nodded. "Are you and my daughter getting along any better now?" he said finally.

The question surprised Thomas, the bluntness of it. "We getting along just fine."

The man sat down in an easy chair. "What about when y'all go out? Anybody say anything to you? Give either of you a hard time?"

Thomas stayed on his feet, looking down at him. This was just what he'd been afraid of. "No. Maybe a few looks from people old as you, but that's all."

He realized the man didn't like his answer from the way he turned his head, and he probably would have preferred a "No, sir."

"What about your friends? They ever say anything to you? Or anything ugly to my daughter?"

"Daddy, leave him alone." Georgine tried to walk between them but there was no room. "I didn't bring him in here for this."

Thomas couldn't hold back then. "So you think my friends going to say something mean 'cause they black? How you know I don't have white friends too? Maybe they the ones saying mean things behind her back."

"I'm just trying to watch out for my daughter. I hope you are too."

"Course I am. You think I don't care about your daughter? I do," he said. "I'll tell you what it comes down to. You don't think any man can care about your daughter, white or black, and that shows just what you think of her."

They walked out then. There was nothing else to say. When they pulled out of the drive, he saw a white man standing in his yard, watching them. He was younger than Georgine's father, maybe not much older than either of them. The man kept staring. Georgine wouldn't look at him. Another cracker, he thought. "You know him?"

"Yeah," she said.

Months later, when they had broken up for what he thought was the last time and her father had come knocking on his door, he hadn't felt like he owed the man anything. So he just let him knock. And how could he have told the man that he didn't care for her anymore, that she had beat down with need whatever feelings he'd had?

The knocking was louder this time, more urgent than before, and well past midnight. David knew it couldn't be because of the baby. The two weeks that had passed wouldn't have made much difference there. He'd heard them arguing earlier, before Thomas left for his shift. Maybe she had found out from Thomas that he'd called her father, and she wanted to confront him now. Or her father had 'fessed up and admitted to her that he'd gotten several calls from that white neighbor of hers. David had even gone by his office once, then gotten some work done on his car that had been beyond his mechanical, and financial, abilities.

She was yelling out his name now and her voice sounded full of fear, not anger, or maybe it was closer to desperation.

"I got to call Thomas," she said when he opened the door. "Somebody just tried to break in my bedroom window." She wasn't crying, but she looked upset, her face pinched tight.

He stepped back from the door and let her in. "Did they break the window?"

"No. I don't know." She kept turning from him, full of nervous energy. "Maybe. I just ran out."

"Did you see a car outside? You think they're still around?"

She shook her head. "I just got to call Thomas and tell him to come home."

He walked into the kitchen with her and handed her the phone. "You ought to call the police first," he said.

She stopped and stared blankly at him as if he had shocked her awake from a dream. "No. I mean he's probably long gone, or they are." She looked even more afraid now, frightened almost to the point of tears, and he somehow felt sorry for her. He believed he could have knocked her over with the lightest touch.

"All right," he said. "Whatever you want to do."

She began to dial. Without saying anything more, he found his flashlight under the sink, turned on the outside light, and walked out his back door. He didn't expect to find anyone, and couldn't believe he was letting himself get pulled into more of her drama, but he shined his light into the strip of woods that lined the back of the yard. His beam hardly penetrated the web of branches and brush. He walked to the far side of the duplex and to the window that sat opposite his own bedroom window. Nothing was broken, not the screen, not the window, and nothing lay on the ground. The grass was too thick to show any footprints. Maybe she had imagined a noise, or wanted to, and amplified it in her head until it reached a point she couldn't stand.

He walked around to the front and was surprised to find her sitting on the top step of the porch. She seemed calm now, as if it was early in the evening and she was waiting for supper to cook and it wasn't almost one o'clock in the morning.

"Did you get him?"

"He'll be home soon."

He sat down next to her. A car passed and turned into a drive toward the end of the street.

"Thomas tell you your father came by a while back?" He knew bringing up her father was a risk. Maybe Thomas hadn't told her.

"Yeah."

"You ever talk to him?"

She was quiet a minute. "No," she said. "Not for a good while. He don't like Thomas too much. Guess you can figure out why."

He nodded. "When he came by here, he didn't say anything mean about Thomas."

"Doesn't mean he didn't think it."

"How'd y'all meet each other, anyway, you and Thomas?" Maybe he was only making conversation, or maybe he actually wanted to know.

"I knew him in school. He was always nice to me. Not many boys were. Then I saw him at the store while I was putting gas in my father's car. I'd lost some weight." She paused a moment. "I guess he noticed. Told me I was looking good. I started meeting him places."

"So your father wouldn't know?"

"Yeah, but I finally told him."

In a few minutes he heard Thomas's truck coming, then the head-lights found them, and he felt caught in the act of something but wasn't sure what.

After opening the store in the morning and waiting on the first customer, who wanted a carburetor for a F-150 pickup, he went into his office and called Georgine's father. When he explained what had happened, the man sounded more than worried. But David told him that maybe no one at all had been at his daughter's window. "She could have imagined it, or even," he hesitated a moment, "made it up." Her father's silence told him that he knew either might be true.

Hours later, when his office line rang, he was surprised to hear the man's voice again.

Thomas hadn't been her only one. There had been others here and there. Boys? Men? Maybe something in between. Mostly she'd known them from back in high school, a few who had once made fun of her. They'd come to her with their need, and she'd obliged them wherever they took her, including the neighbor's house across the street from her father's. But Thomas had wanted something more, which she wanted to trust, but maybe never had. That's what he used to tell her, to just trust him. Then he stopped telling her that, and hadn't now in a long time. She'd never been smart in school, but she knew what his silence meant. Still, compared to Thomas, all the others were just pale boys.

She thought she'd heard a noise the other night. Hadn't she? Maybe she had only wanted to hear one, but that was enough, it turned out, to bring him home, and she'd needed to know she could. He had gone back to work, though, which meant he didn't believe her. Last night, she'd heard it again, loud as a bird crashing into a too-clear pane of glass. It scared her enough that she wet her gown a little. She knew there'd been no point in telling Thomas. Now here she was, lying in bed, tense, waiting for it again. But for what, her own imagination?

Maybe it woke her this time. Three loud bangs. There wasn't any question. Her heart began to pound just as strong as the beats against her window, and her chest felt tight and made of glass. Someone was out there. Kids, a crazy man, some man or boy she'd once been with?

She lay shaking. She had never known anyone could actually shake from fear. It was only in the quiet that came that she found the courage to move. She put her feet to the floor, got up, and pulled on a robe. David might think she was crazy, but he'd listened to her the last time.

It took him longer than usual to answer the door. When he did, his living room was dark and he had on pajama bottoms. He didn't sound as if he had been asleep, though. When she told him what she'd heard, he did not act surprised. "Wait a minute," he said.

After a moment, he was back at the door with a flashlight, no shirt still, and barefoot. He walked down the steps, clearly wanting her to follow him, which surprised her, and she stood on the porch, unsure what to do.

He must have sensed her hesitation. He stopped and turned toward her. "Let's both look," he said, and it sounded important to him that she come. The way he spoke, with no fear in his voice, made her follow.

Once they reached the side of the duplex, he shined his light on the window. The screen was there, not torn or bent. Then he shined his light on the ground and she saw first the blue handle and then the rusty shaft of a screwdriver. Her breath came short and made her chest tighten again. She felt as though the need of her imagination had put the thing there for her to find, but she knew someone's hand had to have dropped it.

He bent down and picked it up. "You want to call Thomas?" he said. He'd pointed the light on himself when he spoke, and she noticed the shine of sweat across his shoulders. He asked the question without any excitement in his voice. Maybe he was trying to keep her calm.

"I guess I should call him. I can tell him what we found," she said, but she felt afraid that a rusty screwdriver wouldn't be enough to bring him home, not this time.

It was much later before she realized neither one of them said anything about calling the police.

When the only black supervisor at the cement plant, Mr. Trimble, came and told him that she was on the phone again, he'd been expecting it. How many calls had she made now?

"This is getting kind of old," Trimble said. "But I tell you, I got family, just like you got coming—or close enough anyway. You been working midnights so long, we might could try moving you to days."

"No, that's all right," he said. "I'll keep on with nights, at least for a while. Don't want to cause no trouble." He hoped the man wouldn't push things. He knew what he said had sounded strange. Nobody wanted midnights.

Once in the office, he listened while she told him about the screwdriver, and he heard in her voice that she didn't expect him to come home. He hadn't been prepared for that, and it somehow made it even harder for him not to go to her when she finally asked, but he didn't give in to her, or to his own feelings.

She was gone when he walked in that morning, and he thought she could be gone for good, scared away. The crib still sat in the corner of their bedroom, but maybe she hadn't had a way to haul it off yet. Then he checked the dresser, and some of her clothes were there, stuffed in, nothing folded. He was disappointed, but there was a kind of relief in that feeling. He knew he could push this, see it through to the end. He only had to wonder how much more time it would take.

While he was eating a bowl of cereal, she came in the door carrying a basket of clothes. "You walked all the way to the laundromat?" He knew that wasn't what he should be asking her about.

"I needed to get out of this apartment awhile. And I needed some clean clothes."

"You wash any of mine?" he said.

"No, I didn't."

She dumped the clothes on the sofa and began to fold them without paying any real attention to what she was doing, and wouldn't look at him when he asked if she'd had breakfast.

"You could of called the police, you know?"

"That wouldn't have done any good."

"How you know?"

"I just do."

He waited for her to turn his way and study him, watch his face for whatever it might tell, but she ignored him, either out of hurt or punishment, or maybe both.

"They would have just walked around with their flashlights," she said finally, "told me whoever it was probably thought nobody was home since there wasn't a car parked on our side."

"You might be right," he said, surprised that she had thought it through that far.

She turned to him now, leveled her gaze at him. "Ain't that what you figured on, if I'd called them?"

He wasn't sure how to answer. "I guess so," he said when she looked away from him and back at her clothes.

She worked for some time, putting more care into what she was doing, even refolding some of the items. He knew it was only an effort on her part not to speak, and it had more of an affect on him than he would have thought. Her silence seemed to enlarge the space between them, allowing his guilt room to grow, and whatever other feelings he might still have for her.

Then she stood sideways to him with a stack of clothes in her hands, and he could see, perhaps for the first time, the new swell that had come into her belly, and maybe for that reason or simply because she turned herself away from him now in a way she hadn't before, he went to her, instead of trying to speak, and put his arms around her shoulders. What he was doing made no sense to him, and yet he did it, and for a moment she let him hold her and he felt the softness of her arms that was too soft. When she slowly twisted away from his hands, her movement out of his grip told him what he'd done made no sense to her either.

Her father hoped for her call, first at home that night, then in his office the next day. But it didn't come. His calling her wouldn't do any good, he knew, and might seem too much of a coincidence. Then he remembered the thought was pointless. She probably still didn't have a phone, not one that was connected. What a way for her to live. No phone, no car, no job, a cheap apartment, and pregnant by a black kid with no future who didn't love her. If he ever wondered that the boy maybe did love her, he didn't now. When David came by and stood in his office and told him it was a go, that Thomas had said yes, that was all he'd needed to hear. As much as he hated it, and he did, he was only doing what he had to. A good father always did, no matter the hurt he felt.

But how many more nights? Every other midnight for almost a week now—still no call to him. And despite all her dumb mistakes, he knew she was smarter than she gave herself credit for. Still, that's why he'd handed David such a wad of bills. If she ever figured it out, she was bound to think it was Thomas's idea, something he'd cooked up with David. At worst, she'd blame David, and Thomas wouldn't know who really came up with the idea. That was why he'd paid David so much, not to tell Thomas what Thomas didn't need to know.

She couldn't leave. There was nowhere for her to go, or almost nowhere. No friends. Not to her mother. And when she thought about her father, she decided she had rather brave the noise at the window. And she did brave it, with a baseball bat she'd made Thomas buy her, and with the knowledge each night that every door and window was locked tight. She braved it with doubt too, a creeping doubt that the noises weren't real, or imagined either, but something else entirely. Maybe the screwdriver hadn't even been real.

A few days ago, she decided she would call the police the next time, but she was into the fourth night of nothing, well past the normal time, and still no sounds anywhere. She had slept some during the day—she'd been doing that a lot—but she thought she might sleep tonight and finally made sure the curtains in the bedroom were drawn tight.

She knew without looking at the clock that dawn was still hours away and that the silence she heard now couldn't have awakened her. Maybe it was pressure from the baby, which somehow she had come to love because it told her that the baby was there, hers, always with her with its need of her body. No one had ever needed her body as much. She imagined it as a boy but hadn't wanted to know when they offered to tell her. She pictured him now, his body small and brown, then standing and taking his first steps, and that was when she saw the upright figure in her doorway like something born large and male out of her imagination.

She didn't scream. No sound would deliver from the contraction of her throat. She didn't move and neither did the dark image whose blank or covered face she couldn't see. Instinctively, she knew it wasn't Thomas. The size and shape were all wrong for him.

He moved then, toward her. She kept her eyes almost closed and wished the bat were in her hand instead of on the floor. She remained still, tried to keep her body from shaking, and watched the figure lean over her and hover as if he were unsure of what he was supposed to do. He sidestepped along the edge of her bed, slowly, then stood and looked around the room. For what?

He turned his back to her and disappeared through the door into a deeper quiet than the one she had awakened to. She waited, unsure herself what to do. Maybe no one knew, in the darkest hours of the morning, what they should do about anything that confronted them.

The quiet stretched out long and thin toward some kind of break-ing point that she waited on. She thought about the bat again, taking it in hand and walking with it into the living room, swinging against a moving shadow and against the quiet, shattering both.

But the quiet snapped on its own into a burst of crashes, metal against metal jarring and rebounding against walls and floors and counters. Then the back door slammed so hard it shook windows, and she lay there, tense, unable to move still.

Finally the quiet returned to normal. She heard a car go by, the tick of the clock beside her bed, and later when she walked toward the kitchen she heard the low hum of the refrigerator. She turned on the light and every pot and pan she'd left drying on the counter lay on the floor, their shining tops scattered among them, mostly upside down.

She looked around the apartment. Nothing was missing, not the television or the small boom box, and he hadn't touched her. It seemed he had come only to make noise, and to carry away with the last of her nerves, which she thought maybe he had done as he'd slammed the back door. But why close it behind him—to keep her from following?

She could go next door, as she had so many times, but she decided that David had done all that he was good for. And Thomas. Maybe they were both good for nothing. She reached her breaking point then, and she poured out of herself, down her thighs and thick bare legs, and puddled the linoleum floor. It wasn't urine this time. She knew that with a certainty she had never experienced.

Just as he hadn't been sure exactly when she'd moved in, David did not see her move out, but Thomas told him outside on their porch, "She's gone," and that was all he said at first. While he'd seen the relief in Thomas's face, he had heard blame in those two words, maybe enough for both of them. There was something else in his expression too that weighted Thomas's features and told him that Thomas was holding back something he didn't want to tell.

"So what about the baby?" he said. "You still going to..." David couldn't finish, but he didn't have to.

"Help take care of it?"

"I guess that's what I mean."

"She's had it, you know."

"No, I didn't have any idea." Somehow it was hard for him to imagine the baby had actually been born.

"Well, it come. But believe me, I ain't got to take care of it."

"All right, man. That's your business, not mine."

Thomas looked at him, and started to speak, but he held himself back again. Maybe it didn't matter that he wouldn't say anything more. Their business together was done. All of it. He hadn't called or heard a word from the girl's father, either, which was probably best.

Weeks went by and when he and Thomas happened to pass each other in front of the duplex, they hardly spoke. Then for three days in a row, he didn't see the low-rider truck, and when he looked through Thomas's partially open blinds, he found that the apartment was empty.

Late one afternoon he sat in his office at the store filling out an order and heard a scraping noise against his door. He looked up and saw Georgine pushing a stroller. What now? he thought. She walked into the office and around his desk, pushed the stroller so close that it bumped his legs. At first she didn't speak but seemed to wait on him, and when he looked down he understood why. The baby's skin was as white as sweet milk, his brown hair so light it was almost blond. David looked up at her and didn't know what to say.

"Yeah, he's mine," she told him. "Beautiful too, huh?" She stared at him.

"He is, but..." He stopped himself. There was no way to ask the question.

"Did I know? That's what you want to ask?" She paused but didn't look away. "Not really. I thought it was Thomas's. I wanted it to be his."

"Are you back at your father's?" What he really wanted to ask was if she was with the baby's father, and who that was.

"For now," she said, and though it sounded as if she had some plan for the future in mind, she didn't reveal it. "You're skinnier than I remember," she added, which seemed to be something she'd been studying closely and felt the need to comment on.

He shrugged and sweat began to form across his face, as if beneath a knitted mask.

"I was going to move out anyway, but not for the reason you might think," she said.

"I wouldn't pretend to know, I don't guess."

She began to gently pull and push the baby's stroller back and forth. The child's eyes closed with the motion. "I doubt that," she said. "It wasn't because I was scared. It's because I know that back door was locked, and didn't nobody break it in. They didn't have to."

He wanted to look away from her, but he wouldn't let himself. Finally, though, he couldn't stand her dark eyes on him. They felt like the eyes of everyone he had ever disappointed. When he looked down at the heavy sleeping child that filled the stroller, he felt thin and empty, as if some essential part of himself had been aborted, and he couldn't have said exactly when.

WATCHING KAYLIE

THE CAR CAME PULLING INTO her drive, too fast. Then she climbed out and stood there, unsteadily, while it backed away and sped off, laughter trailing from the open windows like tattered streamers flashing in the dark. After half a dozen steps, she crumpled into the overgrown yard.

Aaron's first impulse was to run to her, and the pounding of blood against his chest was more than enough to propel him, but he held himself back. What if someone saw? He wasn't stalking her, though, no matter what the neighbors might think, even if they'd seen his truck parked here in the shadows a handful of times these past two weeks.

He stopped thinking and pushed open his truck door, slammed it behind him, and ran across the street to where Kaylie lay. With the trash that was probably running through her veins, she could already be dead, not that he knew how much that would take. He guessed she did, or hoped so.

Once he kneeled down, the light from the streetlamp was bright enough for him to see the smooth rise of her cheekbones, the straight slope of her nose, and the shine of the diamond stud she wore through her left nostril. Her eyes were mostly closed, as if what she dreamed behind them was so much more to her liking than whatever might appear before her. He listened and watched and saw that her breath came regularly. She moved her arms and legs in tandem for a moment, perhaps trying to climb deeper into her waking dream.

Her movements calmed then, her eyes closed, and her breathing remained steady. He reached for the purse she'd dropped and found her keys. After he unlocked the door, he left it open and walked back to her. It occurred to him that she could be worse off than he realized, that maybe he should call an ambulance. But what if she was only drunk? At least someone had driven her home and she hadn't passed out behind the wheel. He had not recognized the car, or any of the voices from inside it.

He slipped an arm behind her neck and worked it down to her shoulders, then put his other arm under her bare legs and lifted. She smelled of perfume and sea salt, though the Gulf was hours away. Maybe this was what he'd been waiting on the nights he'd watched for her. She felt full in his arms, a little heavy, and real to him in a way he'd never experienced before, the warmth of her skin, the softness of her hair. She'd always been a woman with curves, and he liked that—so had his brother, he guessed.

Once he walked into the house with her, he shut the door with his foot, then found a light switch. There were no curtains or blinds on the living room windows. She needed the sunlight, he knew, for when she painted. Other than a few ladder-back chairs and a paint-stained table beside an easel, there was no furniture, no paintings on the walls, except the few turned backwards and leaned against it. All the room seemed to hold was an echo of his steps.

He was hesitant to carry her into her bedroom but found it down the hall and laid her on top of the twisted covers. He started to leave her lying as she was, flat on her back, but he'd heard of people choking on their own sickness, so he managed to roll her onto her stomach, her head still against the pillow. But that position looked obscene to him, the way her thrift-store skirt had ridden up the backs of her legs, exposing the white flesh of her inner thighs, the rise of her buttocks barely covered, or perhaps she simply looked more vulnerable this way, and even more attractive to him. He didn't want to feel an attraction to her at such a moment, though, and realized the obscenity of what stirred within him. He carefully turned her onto her side, took off her shoes, and covered her with the blanket. She appeared more natural now, as if she'd laid down for a nap. He felt better leaving her that way.

Except he didn't leave. He looked through her refrigerator and kitchen cabinets and drawers, found syringes in a zipped compartment of her purse. Over the next couple of hours he checked on her a number of times, and finally couldn't resist turning and looking at the canvases that faced the living room wall. Several were still-lifes of wet grapes piled next to bottles of red wine so dark it looked like blood drawn from a deep vein; some were scenes of either the Black Fork or Tennahpush rivers, their muddy currents pushing against curved banks, and finally he saw one that he hoped he hadn't been looking for without realizing it, a self-portrait of her shadowed face and bare breasts. The nipples were pierced through with thin silver needles and made the painting look unreal somehow, but erotic and disturbing at the same time.

He decided he'd stayed far longer than he should have, that he had entered not just someone's house but a strange place inside himself and knew he had to leave. He leaned the paintings where they'd stood, and without checking on her again, too afraid of how much he might be drawn to her, he walked to the front door and locked it behind him. He crossed the street to his truck, feeling sick with himself, as if he had gone in to her one last time and touched her in some inappropriate way.

He knew that he had never been attractive to women. He was tall, but his height didn't fit him. His body was too thin, gangly, his hands and arms too long and disproportionate. At thirty-eight, even his face had begun to grow long, and his features had always been too small and narrow. He'd tried a beard once, but decided it only made him look older. Maturity hadn't helped much, but there had been women here and there since high school, where there'd been none, mostly ones he met at The Loft, which was the bar he went to out on the highway that had once bypassed most of Demarville but was now lined with fast-food joints and strip malls that stood in what he knew were old cow pastures. The women he met there were always a little more drunk than him, and they never seemed so much willing as hopelessly bored. Usually he would follow them home. They never wanted to let him drive them to where he lived out in the county on the other side of the Black Fork, and there was never a second time. Sometimes he felt his whole life had taken on the narrow line of his body.

Then he met Kaylie. She'd been sitting at the bar, alone, and began talking to him. It didn't take him long to figure out that she knew who he was. She'd been dating his brother Charles and seen pictures of the two of them. This was during the period that he and Charles weren't speaking. They'd opened a small catfish-processing plant, West Alabama Catfish, at home in Riverfield in the Anderson's old cement-block store building. After a year of barely making it, Charles had forced a sale and they'd fallen out over it. When the new owners finally declared bankruptcy, Aaron decided Charles had been right.

Nothing had happened between him and Kaylie that night at the bar, or any other night. Mostly he'd avoided talking about Charles, and himself, which made the conversation awkward and one-sided. What he couldn't figure out was why she was there alone, without Charles. A nurse who chain-smoked seemed a little unusual too. And then she'd left so abruptly, as if she had to go meet someone and couldn't say who.

After leaving her house, he didn't make it home until two o'clock that morning, and kept having visions of her lying in her bed while he tried to find sleep beneath his own covers.

By seven o'clock he'd had several cups of coffee and carried one with him to his truck. He passed the Riverfield post office and the several deserted buildings that surrounded it, including his failed catfish-processing business, and drove on out to the highway that carried people either south to Demarville or north to Valhia, but mostly, it seemed, away from Riverfield.

He owned the Bait Shop now, or what used to be called the Bait Shop. When he bought it, the sign said Gas & Go, so he left it that way, and the old minnow tanks were cracked and filled with junk, anyway. After he opened up and Glory, the black woman he'd hired to work part time, came in complaining about her arthritis, he walked out back to where his brother had set up his trailer beneath a stand of tall pines and knocked loudly at the front door.

"You better close your eyes before you bleed to death," Charles said when he opened the door and looked him over.

"I didn't sleep good."

"No shit."

Charles backed away and let him in, and Aaron sat down at the kitchen table while Charles finished frying bacon at the stove. The popping sound and the smell made him wish he had someone to cook for him.

"What was you doing up so late?" Charles said. "Eating the gun?"

"If I'd ate the gun, I wouldn't be sitting here, would I? I wish you wouldn't say stuff like that to me."

"All right, brother. Maybe you just chewed on it, because something's been bothering you, and, like you say, you ain't dead."

Aaron looked out the sliding glass door behind him, or tried to. The duct-taped cracks in it kept his attention. "Kaylie's gotten into some pretty heavy stuff," he said. "That's what I been hearing, anyway."

"You're being kind of vague."

"Maybe I don't know much about it."

Charles sat down at the table to eat. "You don't need to know any more. Leave it alone, and her."

"You know her father died a couple of months ago. Now the hospital's fired her."

"I didn't know about her being fired. You hadn't told me." Charles stopped eating and looked at him. "I don't want to hear any more."

"You don't care about her at all?"

"Sometimes you're pretty stupid, brother."

"How's that? And how about a little compassion?" he said, not sure if he meant for Kaylie or for himself.

Charles merely shook his head, as if the answer were too obvious to bother with. "You're worse than a blind hog. At least a blind hog will stumble across an acorn now and again. You just can't see what anybody with two eyes and half a brain can see when they look her way."

"What about you? You went out with her."

"I didn't need eyes for what I was looking for. Besides, I ain't as sensitive as you."

Aaron wasn't sure if Charles was making fun of him or not. It was always hard to tell with his brother.

"They say she's taking heroin," he said and watched to see if Charles would react. He knew how dramatic he must have sounded.

"Who says?"

"A couple of people at the bar."

Charles shrugged. "Demarville's a partying town. She's always partied with it."

"So have you," he said and almost brought up the six months Charles had done for possession of marijuana. "But she ain't never partied like this."

Charles stood up and carried his plate to the sink. "No, but she's always been headed there."

Aaron was quiet a minute. Everyone, he guessed, was headed somewhere, and probably someplace different from where they thought. "Reckon where I'm headed?" he said. It seemed like a strange question for him to ask aloud, and he wasn't sure where it came from, unless all the trips into town and back these last nights were his own crooked path and he was a blind hog.

"Not after her, I hope," Charles said. "I been knowing what a thing you got for her." He tucked his T-shirt into his pants. "But all I really know right now is where I'm headed, and that's to Marion driving a gravel truck. Reckon how many car windshields I can crack on the way over?"

"How many do you want to?" he asked, and almost added, you asshole.

Charles laughed. "Not as many as you might think, little brother."

Blue and red neon signs glowed in the windows. He'd always found their light comforting, despite the fact that they illuminated very little and were only advertisement for the brand of beer he held in his hand. He hoped she might come in, though as far as he knew it had been weeks since she'd walked through the door. He didn't want to go to her house again, and told himself he wouldn't. He'd stayed away the last few nights, had come here instead.

Two hours passed through him in what he thought of as liquid time, which might have meant it was closer to three. And then, between the fifth of Jack Daniel's and the quart of Smirnoff, he saw the reflection of her face in the bar mirror and imagined her needle-pierced breasts without trying, though he knew no one could actually wear hypodermic needles beneath a bra, that what he'd seen the other night was just a strange, dark painting, unreal but true enough. When she smiled at him, he decided that this image was real. He knew she'd show at some point.

He picked up his beer and approached her.

When he was close, she leaned toward him and whispered in his ear, "Thank you, Aaron." Her tone sounded heavy with meaning, or maybe drugs or alcohol had simply slowed her words, and the beers he'd drunk had impaired his ability to interpret meaning from them.

"For what?" He was afraid of her answer, of what she might remember.

"For coming over." She pulled back and looked at him. "I could use some company."

"Hadn't seen you in a while," he said, testing her maybe.

"I been in Tuscaloosa over a week, helping my mother with some of my father's things." She took a drink and so did he. He wondered which of them was the better liar. Though maybe she wasn't lying to him but for him, trying to put him at ease with feigned ignorance of what he'd done.

"That long?" He wondered why he questioned her when he knew she was lying.

"Not like I got a job to go to."

"How you making it?" It wasn't something he should have asked, but he meant in general, not how she was paying her bills.

"I sold two paintings in Tuscaloosa."

He knew that didn't mean much money, if she'd really sold something. "You started looking for a job?" He was afraid for a moment that she might say she was moving back to Tuscaloosa.

She either didn't hear him above the music or pretended not to. She lit another cigarette. Then he noticed the stud she usually wore in her nose was missing. He watched her smoke, the feminine way she held her cigarette, and couldn't think of anything to say. He saw then that her fingers were bare. Usually she wore two rings on her left hand, one on her right. There'd been only one pawnshop in town, but with gambling over in Mississippi now, there were at least two others.

"I know you miss your father," he said. There was nothing else to say.

She nodded. "You'd think I might be glad he was gone. He didn't like my paintings, the way I dressed, the guys I went out with. He sure wouldn't approve of me now."

"What do you mean by that?" He was surprised that she would offer any kind of hint about her late recklessness, unless she did remember what he'd hoped she wouldn't.

She turned and looked at him over the top of her beer. "I think somebody went in my house while I was gone."

He tried to act surprised, which was not hard considering the suddenness of what she'd said. "Did they take anything?" he managed to say.

"I don't think so. Just moved some of my paintings around, went through some drawers. Everything's all right. Or maybe I'm imagining it. Maybe I'll become one of those paranoid old women who thinks her neighbors are stealing from her." She looked past him then, as if her mind had drifted toward some sad and distant future.

She asked about Charles, and later how his store was doing. Finally she looked at the clock behind the bar and crushed out her cigarette. "It's late. I need to go," she said.

When she stood, she placed a hand on his shoulder and gently squeezed. He could smell the perfume in her hair and it reminded him of the way her bedroom had smelled, though he hadn't been conscious of any scent that night. "Thank you again," she whispered.

This time he didn't ask for what; he only watched her walk to the door and wondered where she was going, who she might meet, how she'd get home. He finished his beer and paid his tab, and hers.

A week passed and he didn't see her, despite his going to the bar each night, which was about the only place he'd ever seen her. And still he managed to keep himself away from her house, though his desire to watch over her grew along with his deeper desires. One night after erratic sleep, he awoke from a dream where he had tried to remove needles that protruded from all over her breasts. When he sat up in bed, the nerves in his hands stung from where she'd begun slapping at him, and the ends of his fingers burned from each slivered metal jab. She had seemed as real then as when he'd lifted her, and he welcomed the pain.

The next night he parked within shadows of elm trees cast by a distant streetlamp. A little after one o'clock, her car still not in her drive, he began to wonder if someone had brought her home again, before he arrived.

He crept his way to a window and crouched beside a ragged shrub, the shadow of his body a strange creature painted against the house. He looked in and saw that the table and easel were gone, and the paintings he'd seen. The back windows were curtainless too, he found, and the house deserted. Tuscaloosa, he thought. For a moment there was a kind of relief, a burden removed, but only for a moment. Without the burden, he felt weightless, like a shadow dissolved into the early morning's darkness.

People still sometimes stopped and asked for what he couldn't sell them—minnows, crickets, live worms. There'd been two fishermen that morning, and after they left, he walked through the back room and out the door to see if Charles had mowed the grass between the store and the trailer like he'd said he would. He hadn't, and his truck was gone. In fact, he had not seen his brother in several days, not that that was unusual.

He heard music then, coming from the trailer. When he tried the door, it was locked, and Charles had never given him a key. Some fear he didn't want to acknowledge kept him from knocking, and he realized he'd been glad the door was locked.

Between customers, he found himself drawn again and again to his back door, and he watched each time for movement at one of the trailer windows. Finally he saw what he knew he would, a flash of her dark hair, and then her still face looking back at him through the cloudy, sap-stained glass. They stared at each other, and by the time he realized she was naked she had already turned away from the panes that separated them.

He locked his front door and put the "closed" sign in the window at exactly seven o'clock that night, and knew Charles might be home by then.

The music had stopped, he found, and after knocking he heard Charles walk to the door. His brother opened it, stood in the crack, and didn't step away.

"I know you got company," he said.

"Yeah, and I guess you know who."

"So what's going on with her? How long she been here?"

"A few days."

"So what about all that advice you gave me about staying away from her?" he said. "It don't apply to you?"

Charles stepped out and closed the door behind him. "She got evicted from the house she rented."

"I know."

Charles looked at him suspiciously. "How'd you know that?"

"Just heard it," he said.

"Her car's in the shop too. She called me from out on the highway where she'd broke down. I guess I ain't as hard as you think."

"You sleeping with her?"

"It ain't about that."

Aaron looked back toward his store, at the roof that needed replacing. "You didn't answer me."

"Not that it's any of your business, brother, but no."

"I don't think I believe you."

"Believe whatever you want. I can handle this."

"What's that supposed to mean?"

"It means I ain't the one who's in love with her."

"You going to let me in?"

"Aaron, now ain't a good time."

He knew he should walk away. "How come?"

"Just ain't. She's asleep."

He watched his brother, saw that Charles wouldn't look at him now but only beyond him. "She's stoned. You got her high. You been getting her high."

"Look man, this ain't no methadone clinic. She's doing the best she can. Not that I'm saying I got her high. You hear me? I ain't saying that."

"You just bought it for her. You wanting to go back to jail?"

"Hey, don't ask me no bullshit question like that. I ain't done nothing to deserve going back to jail for."

Maybe you have, he thought, but he knew he had no right to judgment.

He kept watching, first his back entrance, then out a back window. Customers became an afterthought. Then late one afternoon, when Glory, his help, had already gone home, he locked his front door and put up a sign that said "Back in an hour" and didn't write down the time. Only God knew how long this might take. Just because he wanted her, had dreams about her, watched her through windows, didn't mean he couldn't help her. There was nothing unseemly about wanting to help someone, whatever the reason. He didn't have to feel guilty about that. Though somehow he did.

No music, this time. After he knocked, he waited for the sound of soft footsteps, but none came. When he tried the door, he found it unlocked and slowly opened it, calling her name. There was no answer. He became afraid then, just as he was when he'd watched her fall in her yard. He walked in expecting to find her lying on the living room or kitchen floor, maybe in the bathroom, naked, her eyes as vacant as a self-portrait that she'd never been able to finish, her life maybe the only thing now complete.

He made his way through the living room. The air was heavy and still, and the walls felt close, the heat almost a wall that had to be walked through. He realized the air conditioner was either turned off or wasn't working and wondered why. He passed beyond the kitchen and into the bedroom, even more afraid now, his heart beating fast, sweat popping out on his forehead. The bed was empty, unmade. He checked the floor on either side of it, then went into the bathroom. Empty too, bare of any sign of her existence.

If he'd come sooner, he thought, if he'd gotten past himself, she might be at his house now, or getting help from the right people. He should have done what his brother hadn't.

But maybe Charles had taken her somewhere. She hadn't walked the ten miles back into town. Someone had carried her out of Riverfield, one way or another, and he'd missed seeing who, unless she'd hitchhiked. He hated to imagine she would do that and not come to him first. Perhaps, though, there was another answer, one he couldn't let himself imagine, or any part in it that Charles might have played.

At closing, his brother stood there in front of the counter, his feet spread, hands on hips, his attitude clear. "So what did you think happened, Aaron? Damn. You think I carted off her dead body?"

"I didn't know. All I know is, she's gone."

"Damn right she is. And whoever came and got her didn't just take her."

"What else?"

"I knew better. Guess I got what I deserved. Not only did they take my damn stereo," Charles said. "They took the fucking copper coil right out of my air conditioner."

"Why?"

"They can sell it. Why else?" He shook his head in disgust. "I'm done with her. If she calls you, hang up."

She had never called him. For a moment he imagined her voice on the line saying his name, needing him. He knew then that he hoped she would.

After opening the next morning, he drove into town and out to the highway to see if her car was still in the shop. He paid a man behind the counter whose hands were dark with grease, then said, "She'll be in to get it."

"Yeah," he said and turned away, as if he knew her and had his doubts.

He wanted to search for her, but there was no place to begin. She'd disappeared into a world he didn't know, one that couldn't even be glimpsed in the light of day, and that left night and no house to watch. And where was her furniture, her paintings? All sold cheap probably, or in some storage unit that soon enough would be locked against her. His best guess was that she was on someone's filthy couch, or in their bed. And if he did begin to ask around and was somehow able to find her, what would he do? He didn't see her leaving with him, and he couldn't drag her away. The people she was with were thieves, or worse. Wherever she was, he would bet that there were guns. Charles had been right, but being right and knowing someone was right didn't really mean all that much sometimes.

For a week he stayed away from town. He tried not to think about her, and if she entered his dreams he wasn't able to hold onto her once he awoke, until one morning when he remembered a dream he wished he hadn't. She lay flat on her back. Her face was pale and her eyes shut. He looked down the length of her body and saw that she was naked, her breasts pooled toward either side, drops of blood at each pierced nipple, and needle marks down her arms. He heard music, and somewhere within it, her voice, but her words were indistinguishable and her lips didn't move. It was only when he woke that he realized he'd been looking at her corpse, and wherever she lay, he felt somehow that he had placed her there, just as he'd once placed her in her bed.

✳

He went back to the bar, but instead of going in he sat in his truck in a corner of the parking lot, and watched. She might show at some point. There wasn't any reason for her to avoid the place. He couldn't imagine her really caring if she ran into him or not.

After an hour of watching he realized people might see him sitting there and think it strange. He had to make himself give up the comfort and quiet of his truck cab, and the idea that something as simple as opening a truck door had become suddenly difficult made him wonder if all those nights alone, watching for Kaylie, had taken their toll on him in a way he didn't fully understand. Finally he got out, walked through the thick heat and up the stairs, then went inside.

Four nights in a row he sat at the bar and watched the door open and close, his expectation somehow more difficult to handle than each disappointment. When he saw her, it wasn't a surprise. She was thinner but didn't look wasted, as he'd feared. Maybe he'd seen too many movies, their high drama of an addict's life a lie against the low reality.

She sat down at the end of the bar closest to the door. When she looked up and saw him, she waved, slowly, noncommittally. He wasn't sure what to make of it, but he went to her, sat down, and signaled for another beer. She kept studying the mirror behind the bar.

"Your car's ready, you know?" he said.

"Yeah, I figured."

"I mean it's paid for," he said.

She nodded but didn't say another word. Her silence meant embarrassment, he thought, or maybe she'd reached a point where so much bad had happened that she felt an entitlement to anything good that came along.

"If you don't have your car, how'd you get here?" he asked.

"Walked."

"You live close by?"

She looked at him now. "Close enough." A long pause, then she added, "Surprised you hadn't come over for a visit."

He felt as if she had just said to him, *I know your secret.* He wished for a moment that he had never looked for her. "What does that mean?"

"Nothing." She looked away from him, then back. "Just that I'd be glad to see you anytime."

He knew that he'd heard her correctly, but still the words didn't seem real. One moment she sounded almost angry, the next inviting.

"You live with someone?" he said.

"Yeah, several people."

"Who?"

"Different ones. They come and they go."

"Don't you want out of that?" he said and knew they both understood what that meant.

She shrugged, as if the question couldn't be answered.

"You might come stay with me," he said. "For as long as you want." He surprised himself with the words he spoke, but perhaps knowing what she would say in response took away whatever risk he might have felt. "Or as long as it would take," he added.

Her body seemed to sink farther down onto her barstool, as if the idea of moving anywhere from this one spot was more than she could think about. "That's a nice offer," she said. "But you know what happened when I stayed with Charles."

"I could find a place for you, where they know how to help."

She shook her head slowly, with a finality that made him afraid for her and seemed like an answer that was larger than the implicit question.

"You're sweet," she said, "too sweet for your own good."

Her words didn't sound like a compliment but something meant to push him away, and he didn't know how to answer.

"Charles still mad at me?" she said.

"Pretty much."

"I figured. He'd probably be mad at you too if he knew you were sitting here talking to me." She sipped her beer.

He found he no longer wanted his. After some time she seemed to notice that he wasn't drinking. She didn't comment but kept looking around the bar, as if she were searching for someone in particular. He thought that she grew more and more anxious, afraid even. "You meeting somebody here?" he asked her finally.

"What? No. Look," she said, "since you're not drinking, why don't we go outside?"

He felt she was trying to sound casual, but he heard something else in her voice. "Is there someone here you're worried about?"

"Can we just go outside?"

He paid the tab and followed her. As they descended the metal stairs, he felt the rust on the railing and thought about the times he'd left with other women. He knew this wasn't like that, but he still felt anxious somehow, worried that he'd do or say the wrong thing and she would walk away.

"Is there somewhere I can take you?" he said. "Have you eaten any supper?"

"We can just sit in your truck."

He wasn't sure what to make of that, but he led her to the corner of the lot where he'd parked. When he walked her around to the passenger door, she was close enough for him to smell her perfume, but she wore none, and the only scent he detected was the strong smell of cigarette smoke on her clothing.

She didn't speak at first when he climbed into the cab. They sat there with their windows open, acrid dust blown from the highway drifting in and settling.

He realized she wanted something from him, and what it had to be. That was why she was silent. Her fear kept her from asking. If he gave her money, they both knew what she would do with it.

"Aaron," she said and leaned his way, "you're a better man than your brother. You know that don't you?"

"I'm not so sure," he said, surprised that she would say such a thing to him, but glad for it. "He handles things better than I do."

She was quiet again for a moment. "Do you mean he handles me better?"

He didn't answer, because that was exactly what he'd meant, and he wondered how she knew. Perhaps it wasn't hard to figure out.

"You're probably right about that," she said, as if he had answered her, "but he should have known better."

"He did. Sometimes people have to do what they know they shouldn't."

"Guess I'm a good example of that," she said. "And you know better than to take me in, don't you?"

"Probably." He waited on her to ask why he offered, but she didn't, and he felt that he knew why she didn't. "You've seen me, haven't you? And you remembered. I hoped you wouldn't."

She leaned away from him and didn't speak but seemed to be gathering herself for something she had to say or do, maybe something she knew was wrong but had to do anyway, and for more reasons than one. Her eyes were shadowed and appeared filled with a sorrow much larger than what she might have felt for herself only.

"I need money," she said. "You know that. I'll trade you for it."

"What are you talking about?" he asked, but he already knew.

"A trade. Right now. I know you've wanted me."

"Whoever you were looking for up in the bar, you that desperate to pay them?"

"Come on, Aaron. I can take care of you right here."

He closed his eyes into his own sober, waking dream, one he'd had many times. But what he saw now in that internal darkness was himself standing outside of the cab looking in at Kaylie and himself locked in an awkward and strained embrace, each of her movements pushing at him as he reached and reached toward her, his fumbling no more satisfying than with any other woman. But it was a dream, and he shook himself from it. Because here she was, beside him, offering herself, with no stained and dirty window pane between them, only the thin barrier of a transaction, and to say *no* left him only where he had always been, looking, watching, wanting entrance, afraid of the price he would pay if he didn't break through in any possible manner. So what if the moment was tainted. How many pure moments were we ever given, anyway?

He felt her anticipation, her waiting on him, but she didn't push, didn't move toward him. Then, finally, in a slow, easy movement, she pulled herself away, and he saw, or imagined, a look of disgust on her face that could have been for herself or for him, or perhaps it was the disgust she imagined he'd felt for her at her offer—one that was meant to push him away and toward something, or someone, else.

They each remained quiet and didn't move, and the time that passed was answer enough, he decided, for the both of them.

Finally she leaned across the seat and kissed him on the cheek. "You see, I told you that you were a good man." She opened her door then, climbed from the cab, and walked out across the open field beyond the edge of the gravel parking lot, the sound of her footsteps fading.

He watched her disappear and tried not to wonder about where she was headed, or at the kindness she had done him.

SHORT DAYS, DOG DAYS

I DON'T CARE WHAT PEOPLE READ in the paper, I never did call it a flying saucer. And I ain't calling it one now. People are saying I've lost my mind, what there is left of it to lose. That's their joke on me. I know. My wife's told me. Sometimes I think I'm her joke. And my lesbian daughter's.

The thing never did make any noise. All I heard was my dogs, Larry and Jack, barking. They made such a racket that I went out with my shotgun and a flashlight. First I thought it might be a possum or a coon walking around the pen, teasing the dogs. They'll do that sometime. But both Larry and Jack were looking up and baying like they had something treed in that one big water oak that grows in their yard. The thing is, that didn't make sense. The only way anything could get treed in there was to break *into* the pen. I looked up and shined my light anyway.

That's when I saw it hovering. It was kind of glowing, but hardly putting out any light at all. I can't tell you how big it was exactly. Maybe a hundred feet across, and round. No wings on it, none that I could see. It just sat there, or maybe it was spinning. I felt like I was being watched, me and the dogs. Then it dropped, fast, was probably fifty feet off the ground. Larry and Jack really went at it then, not baying like when they tree something, but like when another dog wants to fight. They didn't let up, and I swear the glowing got brighter and maybe it dropped lower and spun faster, because suddenly the air was twisting all around me. That's when I shot at it. First one barrel, then the other one, double-aught buckshot.

The strange thing is, I never heard the buckshot hit anything. I might as well have been shooting at stars. And the next thing I knew, that's what I was looking at. It was gone. I don't mean it flew away. The thing disappeared so fast I didn't even see it disappear.

I stood there a few minutes, not moving, just looking up with my mouth probably hanging open. The dogs got quiet then, settled down in front of their house like nothing had happened. I guess it's all the same to them, a coon or a fox, a strange dog, some machine hovering over them. Once it's gone, they can put it out of their minds and go back to licking themselves.

Things didn't work out quite like that for me.

When I walked back inside, Lois was sitting on the sofa in the den, her housecoat closed up around her. "What was you shooting at?" she said. Sounded like she said it just to say something that wasn't part of the argument we'd been having before the dogs interrupted.

Maybe I was still so confused that I didn't think. Instead of mumbling something about a coon, I told her what I'd seen. That thing must have taken my brain with it.

"You're not very funny," she said. Sounded like the argument was creeping back into her voice.

"I'm not trying to be funny."

She quit picking at the button on her housecoat. "You're seriously wanting me to believe you saw a flying saucer?"

"I saw *something*. I swear."

"And shot at it?

"You heard the gun," I said.

"Maybe you shot just to be shooting."

"Why would I do that?"

"You're so sick of arguing that you're making up crazy shit to shut me up."

"Now there's an idea," I said. "I'll have to remember that. Of course it doesn't seem to be working too good right now. *Not* that I'm making this up, even if it does sound like crazy shit to you."

"What else could it sound like? And if there are flying saucers, why would one fly over the dog pen?"

She stared at me a minute and shook her head. Then she got up and walked into the kitchen in those ratty blue slippers that match her housecoat. Looked like she had something in her mind, or up her sleeve. So I followed her. The land line sits on the kitchen table, and she reached and pulled the book out from under it, took a seat and started flipping pages.

"Who are you gon' call?"

"The sheriff, that's who."

"No you ain't neither."

"He lives just down the road, so it won't take him long to get here. He needs to know we're being invaded."

"Put the phone down."

She started dialing, figuring to call my bluff, I guess. I reached over and jabbed my finger onto the cut-off button.

"What are you doing?" she said. "Don't you know this is too important a thing not to call the authorities? They'll want to bring in scientists and government officials. Of course, it'll all be top secret. Now, did you get taken aboard by spacemen? 'Cause if you did, doctors might want to take your brain out and study it. Or maybe your brain is already missing and those little green men used your empty head as a slop jar."

I wanted to jerk the phone out of her hand, and if she'd kept on I might have.

"Just admit to me that you didn't see no damn flying saucer out there and I'll hang up."

"I'm sorry, but I saw something hovering over the dog pen," I said. "I'm not lying, and I ain't crazy, and I don't want nobody to know my business." I was about yelling.

What she did next surprised me. She actually hung up the phone. Then she marched into the bedroom. I didn't think she'd give up that easy.

"Quit following me," she said when I came after her. "I'm too tired to keep doing this tonight. I've had enough."

I should have known that was a lie.

We'd been arguing earlier about moving into town. She wanted to. I didn't. This wasn't nothing new. She'd been pushing for it two years. First she said it would be better for Margaret, our daughter, who was still in high school. Said she'd be closer to her friends, would make it easier for her to go places with them. What she really meant was that she wouldn't have to drive Margaret into Demarville all the time, or let Margaret use her car.

All this was before Margaret turned into a lesbian. Lois says I make it sound like Margaret's a monster when I say that. Like I might as well go around telling people that she *turned into* a werewolf, when I'm really the one who turned into a monster, according to Lois.

After I told her moving into town for Margaret wasn't a good enough reason, she started talking about how everybody else around here was already moving. And she was right about that. Boys I grew up with, the ones I thought would never leave, like Carter Finley and Willie Green and Bobby Turner, they're gone, raising their kids in town, living in big brick houses. Some people here when I was coming up you just knew would move off, way off, when they got grown. I say *they* never counted.

And so many of the ones who hadn't moved off are in the graveyard now. I'm only forty-five years old and it seems like I know more dead people than live ones. And the dead ones were better people by a damn sight, like old Mr. Anderson who owned the store by the post office. He was honest as the day is long. The way I see it, we ain't got nothing but short days now. His old store just sits empty, with weeds and bushes growing up all around it. Only stores left around here are out on the highway, and if you want more than cigarettes, beer, or gas, you better go to town, 'cause you ain't gon' find it here.

So then Lois said, "What about the crackheads and meth freaks?" And she's right. They're some out here now, blacks and whites both.

Blacks on crack, rednecks on meth, and some of them homegrown too, making it in trailers that sit on land their granddaddies used to farm and sweat over. But I told her, "They got all that in town too. You can't get away from it." Besides, I ain't letting dopeheads run me off. Some good people got to stay.

Lois shook me awake. "The sheriff's at the door," she said.

Took me a minute to figure out, or remember, what was going on. "Damnit, I can't believe you called him."

"I didn't. I swear." She pulled her housecoat tight around her again, like she was cold, or telling a stone cold lie.

"If you didn't call, why's he here?"

"Maybe somebody heard the shots."

I pulled on some jeans and a shirt as fast as I could. "People who live in the country don't call the law just because they hear a gun go off."

"They might with things the way they are out here these days."

"Bullshit," I said, which turned out to be a mistake.

It was the sheriff at the door, sure enough. He stood there in full uniform with his hat in his hand. "We got a call about shots being fired," he said.

His name was Cook. He was only the second black sheriff we've ever had, but the white people had got used to him, and liked him. I noticed he didn't say why it took him so long to get here, or who had called.

"There was maybe just some animal around my dog pen," I said. "I wanted to run off whatever it was."

"You think it could have been some*body*?"

I was trying to decide if I ought to tell him to come on in, so I didn't answer quick as I should have.

"It might have been little green men," Lois said. She'd slipped up behind me. Now she poked her finger into my back real hard. "Don't tell me *bullshit*," she whispered.

The sheriff looked like he didn't know if we were drunk, stoned, crazy, or having a domestic dispute, which I've heard can be pretty dangerous for a cop.

"He says he saw a flying saucer."

"That ain't what I said." I might have been looking at the sheriff, but it wasn't him I was talking to.

"What exactly did you see?" he asked me then, real calm, like this was a regular kind of thing for people to report.

There wasn't any way out of it, so I described the thing as best I could.

"Let's go take a look around your dog pen," he said.

I didn't see much point in it, but we walked on through the house. I picked up my flashlight. He took his off his belt.

"I know you've never heard anything this crazy," I said once we got outside.

He laughed a little. "You got no idea."

When we walked into the pen, the dogs nosed around him some. There wasn't really anything for him to see. At least I didn't think so at first. But I spotted where some old leaves had been blown around in a way that didn't look natural. I didn't say anything. I only wanted him to go. For all he knew, the dogs had been digging in the leaves.

He shined his light up at me, not right in my face, but close enough where I didn't like it too much. "Why'd you shoot at it?" he said.

I didn't want to say, "Because it scared the shit out of me." So I told him how it had been upsetting Larry and Jack.

He dropped his beam. "No law against shooting a gun out in the country."

"Let me ask you something," I said. "My wife call you?"

He raised his light back up, on my face this time. "Like I said, somebody called in shots being fired. Would have been here sooner, but I was out on the road up north of Valhia." He finally lowered his light a little. "You got a daughter, don't you?"

Now I put my light on him, almost in his face. "Yeah."

"She home? She see anything?"

"No, she moved into town, Demarville, about six months ago."

I thought I saw him smile a little, like he just remembered something funny.

When I got home Thursday afternoon from working at the fertilizer plant, there my daughter sat in the living room with my wife. The weekly paper out of Valhia was spread across the coffee table in front of them.

"Hey, Daddy," Margaret said, like I wasn't about to step into a number two steel trap. Her brown hair looked like she'd just got it cut at a men's barbershop by a drunk barber. It used to be long and full—like her mama's.

Lois started reading from the paper, running her finger across the words. "When Mr. Miller was asked why he shot at the flying object, he responded, 'It was worrying my dogs.'" Her and Margaret started laughing hard. They'd probably been laughing all afternoon. "*Hit was worryin' my dawgs*. I can hear you now," Lois said.

I stood there a minute, like I did after that thing had disappeared back behind the stars, not hardly believing it was all in the paper for everybody to see. My legs felt weak, my stomach too. But the worst of it was them laughing, especially my daughter, who used to think her daddy was the greatest man in the world. Now men in general, and maybe me in particular, don't count for much in whatever world she lives in.

They finally calmed down, but something hit me then that hurt worst of all. "I guess you called the paper and told them all about it," I said to Lois. "Every little detail. You must have been at the back door listening that night."

"I didn't tell the paper nothing," she said.

"Just like you didn't call the sheriff?"

"I didn't do that either. I told you."

Margaret stood up. She was always a little on the stocky side, but looked like she'd lost a few pounds since she moved out, which kind of worried me in a way, strange as that may sound. She propped a foot on the table and leaned toward me. I could see the tattoo on her arm that says *Blah! Blah! Blah!*, which I guess is supposed to be all the men of the world talking. First time I saw it, I told her it made her look like a convict at Kilby, the men's prison. That's when Lois said I was a monster. I know I sounded like a jackass, but a jackass only eats hay. They don't spit fire and leave dead bodies in their trail.

"I asked Mama, and she told me she didn't call the paper or the sheriff. She wouldn't lie to me."

"Wish I could believe it, but how else would the paper have known?"

"They look at the police and sheriff's reports every week, Daddy. You know good and well they always list in the paper everybody that's been arrested, and what they've done."

I couldn't believe she'd thrown that up at me. Years back, they listed me in there for theft, stealing a calf, but all I'd done was hold it ransom—until the man's sorry-ass son brought my daughter's bike back that he'd stole out of our front yard. What he wanted with a girl's bike, I don't know.

They had me in there for mayhem once, too. But I did not eat that man's dog. If I'd only kept my mouth shut, but that's a whole other story.

"I didn't get arrested, though," I said, "not this time."

"You're not listening."

I sat down in a chair and pulled my boots off, wondering how many times I'd heard that. I saw the television was on one of those afternoon talk shows, the kind where somebody comes on and talks about their face lift or their combination boob job and penis enlargement and how much better their life is now and everybody applauds. Then they talk about how they wouldn't have ever had that drug problem that almost killed them if they'd only gotten their sex-change operation a little sooner.

"So did you come over to hear your mama read that article to me?" I said.

"No, Daddy. Mama told me about what happened, but I didn't know about the article. Is it so hard for you to believe that I just wanted to come home?" She glanced at her mama real quick, and as soon as their eyes met I knew something was going on.

"Are you planning on staying for supper? You hadn't in a long while," I said.

"I can't. I got some things to take care of."

"Like go out and tell all your friends how your daddy shoots at spaceships that worry his dawgs?"

"No, now that it's in the paper, I won't have to," she said, or mumbled really.

Her mother laughed again.

"I guess you been burning up the phone lines," I said to Lois.

"I might have made a few calls since the other night, and a certain subject might have come up. 'Course the phone's rung a few times today since the paper's come out. You're a celebrity."

I looked at the television screen. A man and a woman were slapping at each other and a big guy was pulling them apart. "Yeah, I'm what everybody wants to be," I said.

After supper I fed Larry and Jack and was sitting on the back porch watching them eat. Lois came out and sat beside me. She stared at the woods awhile without saying much. Then I asked her what Margaret had come over for.

"I figured we'd come around to that sometime tonight," she said. "I was just waiting till you were ready."

"So what's going on?"

She looked at me like I was some cripple in a wheelchair. "She's got her a girl that's moved in with her, and I ain't talking about just a roommate."

I watched Jack jump onto the roof of the doghouse. He likes to stand up there. Larry started barking at him, wanting him to get down 'cause he can't jump up.

"I didn't think about something like this happening. Not yet, anyway."

"Why not?"

"She's too young. And it ain't even been a year since she told us the way she is."

"You mean since she 'turned into' a lesbian?"

"That ain't what I said."

"You been knowing just as long as me that she's the way she is, and that's been way more than a year."

"No I hadn't either. I've told you that. I didn't know until you sat me out here and told me."

"Bullshit, Miller. You ain't as stupid as you sound."

"Hell, she had dates with boys."

"Which didn't mean much."

I didn't say anything for a minute, just watched the dogs. "Where'd she meet her?" I said finally.

"At the beauty school. The girl's mother owns it."

"Great. Ain't they from California?"

"Yeah. And I got something else to tell you."

"What now?"

"Margaret wants to bring her out here for supper one night."

"No way. I can't have that. That's too much for me. I mean it, Lois. You better hear me."

"Guess you don't want to see this, then." Before I knew what she was doing she reached into her shirt pocket, pulled out a picture, and stuck it in front of me. It was one of Margaret standing in front of a tree with her arm around a tall blond girl, real tan, that you'd never guess in a million years was that way. She could have been a model.

"Looks like Butch and Sundance," I said. "They gon' start them a gang?"

Lois stood up and leaned over me. "You're a shit, Miller. Pure and simple."

About midnight was when the dogs started carrying on again, sounding like they had something treed. I hadn't even been asleep, and I grabbed my flashlight and gun, like before.

When I made it to the pen, Larry and Jack were still baying. I looked for the glow first, then waited to see if I could feel the air twisting. I finally shined my light, but there wasn't nothing there. The dogs, though, they kept right on, like something from some other world was up above us, and just because I couldn't see the thing didn't mean it wasn't there. Maybe it was making high-pitched noises that only dogs could hear.

I started to shoot straight up but decided not to waste shells. You can't shoot or fight what you can't see. So I stood beside the dogs with my head thrown back, looking hard as I could, and probably looked like a fool, too, but at least I wasn't barking mad.

Then the dogs stopped, like somebody'd hit them in the throat at the same time. They were still a minute, and Larry went in their house and Jack jumped on top of it again. I walked over and petted him, maybe to calm myself down as much as him.

I didn't want to go back inside. Since I was already in the doghouse with Lois, I decided I'd just sleep outside with the dogs. I could keep watch on them, and on the piece of space above their pen. So I laid out in the hammock at the edge of the yard, hoping the canvas wasn't too rotten to hold.

Sleeping outside's nothing new for me. I call it going to the Green Hotel. I'll take a pack with a little food and a sleeping bag, some matches and a lock-blade knife. If it's hunting season I'll carry my shotgun. Sometimes I'll be gone a couple of days.

Staying in the Green Hotel was what got me my mayhem charge. One night I settled in close to a camphouse on the Tennahpush River that I didn't know was there, and this mix-bred hound must have smelled me. He started to barking and carrying on, and I couldn't sleep. Finally he got real bold and came up so close I could see him. I'd had enough by that time, and I jumped up cussing and hollering so loud my voice echoed back from across the river. I must have sounded like a crazy man, and I know people heard.

Since I was in an agitated state of mind, I did something I wouldn't ordinarily do. I hit the dog with a pinecone, one that was still green. The dog yelped like I'd scalded him and took off toward the river. I don't know where he went from there, but he was gone. Next morning a man come looking for him. Sounded like he was some damn lawyer from Birmingham. Wanted to know if I'd seen his dog. He kept looking from me to my fire to my knife and frying pan. I must have looked like the wild-man-in-the-woods, and I could tell he thought I was crazy enough to have done it. So I said, "Maybe I ate him," and picked my teeth with the point of my knife. A few weeks later he found some bones, but by the time everybody figured out they were from a fox, I'd already been charged. Lois and Margaret were so proud.

I found the man's dog a month later. I named him Larry.

I couldn't sleep in the hammock. Finally I crept inside, got what I needed, and climbed over our fence. Tore my pants while I was doing it. I walked on into the woods, and about one o'clock in the morning found a high spot, built a fire, and settled in. Since I didn't have to work the next day, I could stay as long as I wanted. I watched the stars and tried not to think about wives who turn on you, or daughters who turn away from you.

By the time I got home the next afternoon, Lois had pulled her own disappearing act. The note she left was on the kitchen table. *You run off again you son of a bitch.*

I knew I'd messed up, but not how bad. I wasn't sure what to do, so to pass the time I gave the dogs a bath and dipped them for fleas. I felt guilty about it later. Figured Lois would say I cared more about the dogs than her or my daughter.

I ate supper alone, and slept in the bed the same way, or tried to sleep, that is. Never did hear her car pull in or the door open. The dogs were quiet too, all night.

At work people kept pointing imaginary shotguns in the air and pulling the trigger every time I drove by on my forklift. And at lunch one old boy named Moose who had a long memory asked me if I was eating a dogmeat sandwich. I put up with all that, didn't say much. Mostly I wondered if Lois would be home when I got there. I knew I could call Margaret and find out probably that Lois was with her, but figured that's what Lois wanted.

Sure enough, the house was dead as a graveyard when I got there. I'd have to tough it out at least one more night. Strange thing is, home didn't feel right. It was like strangers had come in and rear-ranged everything, except it all looked the same, and then set the house down on some street in a town I'd never been in. I was almost afraid to look out a window.

Larry and Jack started up at a quarter after two, baying and carry-ing on. I almost jerked the covers off and ran out there again, but told myself the hell with it. For all I cared right then the son of a bitches could land, come on in the house, and fix them some dogmeat sandwiches. If Larry and Jack had kept their mouths shut, maybe none of this would have happened.

The next morning, when I walked out back, both dogs were gone. First I looked inside their house just to be sure, but the only thing in there was the hay I'd put in for bedding. Then I checked to see if they'd dug under the fence. But no holes. Nothing. And the gate had been latched when I'd come through. They hadn't slipped out of it. They were just gone, disappeared, and I felt sick to my stomach. How much can a man take? I thought. I wondered if that thing had come all the way down to the ground this time and stole Larry and Jack. Maybe the thing was real enough to have done what I was thinking, but trying to get my mind around the notion about stretched it to the snapping point.

Lois could have come and turned the dogs out. I didn't want to think that about her, but I started calling and went to looking for them in the woods. After two hours of not seeing or hearing anything but my own voice, I quit. If they'd found some way out of the pen that I'd missed, or if Lois had let them out, they'd be gone for days, hunting till they dropped. Hounds will do that. I could find them later, like I'd found Larry.

That's what I told myself, anyway.

After work that day I went home to my empty house and just sat—didn't watch television, didn't go outside, didn't hear the Green Hotel calling. Instead of worrying about my dogs, all I could think about was Lois. I knew she wouldn't have come after me in the woods for anything, but I was going to have to go after her in town if I wanted her back. She might tell me everything I didn't want to hear, but at least I could count on her to do that, all the way down to calling me a shit. Seemed like she was all I could count on. And if she'd let the dogs loose, I could forgive that.

I'd helped Margaret move into town, so I knew where her apartment was. When I got over there that evening and was about to knock on the door, I heard voices. They stopped when my knuckles hit wood. It took a minute, but Margaret opened the door and stood there. I looked past her but didn't see Lois or any blond girl in the living room.

"I'd like to talk to your mama if I can," I said.

"You all right, Daddy?"

Her question took me aback a little. Something in the way she asked made me feel like I must not be. "Well enough," I said. Before I asked if she was going to let me in, she stepped out and closed the door behind her. Then she walked over and leaned against the hood of my truck. I did the same.

"This is the first time you've come over for a visit," she said. "But this isn't really a visit, is it?"

"I guess not," I said and looked away.

"I'd like it if you came by sometime. If you wanted to."

"I'll have to think about that," I said.

The hurt on her face made me feel like a jackass spitting fire, or some other kind of animal that doesn't really live in the world.

"It's nothing to think about, Daddy. You either come or you don't."

I nodded. It was all I could do.

"Mama's not sure yet," she said.

"About what?"

"Going back home, or about you."

"Let me talk to her," I said. "Tell her I said please."

She went inside, and I stood there feeling like the whole world was watching me.

Lois finally came out. Seemed a little like they were tag-teaming me, but I could see why. "What brings you to town?" she said. She stood across the truck from me. "I know how much you hate it here."

"You let my dogs out?" I said, except it wasn't what I meant to say at all.

"What?"

"My dogs are gone."

"I'm tired of being accused of things. And hell no I didn't let your dogs out. Maybe you ate them and forgot. You know you ate Larry once. Maybe you ate him again."

I let that pass. I believed her, though, and believed that she hadn't called the sheriff or the paper either one. Maybe it was something in her tone, or it could be that I just needed to believe her, finally, because everything else seemed too damn unbelievable.

"Maybe your spaceship got them."

"I heard it again, or at least heard the dogs barking at it."

"Damn, Miller. The only place that thing flies is inside your head. And the dogs will turn up."

"So have you moved into town permanent, like you been wanting?" I didn't really think she had, but I had to ask.

"I don't know," she said. "I do know I can't stay here much longer. I'm crowding them." I almost rolled my eyes, and she must have expected me to. "Leave it alone, Miller. She does got her own life."

"And you?"

"My life's been with you for a lot of years. Like I said, I don't know."

"What do I need to do?"

"That's for you to figure out."

I wanted to cuss. But I didn't use any bad language, or ask any more questions. I don't think she expected me to be that smart. She kept looking at me like she was afraid something stupid was about to come out of my mouth. Sometimes all you can do with a woman is not say anything.

"I've got to go back inside," she said. "I'm fixing them some supper."

"The girl in there?"

"Her name's Cameron. And no, she ain't. She'll be home after a while."

"You like her all right?"

"Yeah, I like her all right. But mostly I love our daughter."

The dogs stayed gone that night, and the house felt even stranger than before, like all the clocks were telling a different time and the crazy people on television were about to climb through the screen and start talking to me in my dreams.

Early the next evening, Margaret came pulling up to the house. I'd called, said I'd fry some catfish in the big pot outside. I didn't say anything about her mama, and she didn't either. 'Course I hoped it would make Lois happy that I'd asked Margaret over, but that ain't why I did it.

Margaret stopped the car, and the setting sun glinted strong off the windshield. She opened her door and walked around to the passenger side. I figured she'd brought some food. When the blond girl, Cameron, got out, it was everything I could do to keep from shaking my head and closing my eyes. Margaret was looking, probably expecting that from me. Maybe that's what kept me from doing it. Then Margaret took the girl by the hand. She's got guts like her mama, I thought.

I walked toward them. Way off in the woods, I heard a dog bark.

PLAYING WAR

THE ALABAMA BLACK BELT in late fall is an abstract painting. The rusts and yellow-browns of broom sedge across a hill are merely the sure sweep of hard brush strokes, the pines and cedars thick smears of green paint. Twists of gray bones rise into shapes that might be oaks, sweet gums, and maples. Creeks are dark, narrow lava flows. And when Carrie Fuller drives slowly down the blacktop of a county road and sees the landscape in this manner, it seems timeless but removed from her somehow, not a part of her world. The vision always, finally, fails her, though. She knows too well what happens in the woods.

It isn't that the seasonal killing of deer bothers her—she's lived among hunters all her life—but pulling up behind a pickup with its tailgate down and seeing a buck lying slack in the bed, its antlers and head twisted at an odd angle, its pliant tongue hanging out, kills the abstraction she wants, the abstraction that protects her from images worse than those of dead deer.

She crosses over the muddy current of the Black Fork River, having left her father's house in Riverfield, and soon passes into the city limits of Demarville. She finally pulls into her driveway and feels the small sense of surprise that still comes on her when she looks up at her own home. It's as if the house isn't really hers; she's allowed to stay here but isn't sure if she should. The house is two-story and so much larger than what she grew up in, or ever dreamed of calling home. Her husband, Foster, tells people it was built with asphalt, meaning the paving company he started from scratch paid for every square foot. What little money she makes doesn't count for much now, it seems, but early on it fed them.

He's home, somewhere; his truck is parked in the drive. Once in the bedroom, she slips out of the white uniform she wears at the dentist's office and pulls on a T-shirt and jeans over the good figure she's struggled to keep. She's tired, even though she works only part time now. Foster has told her for years that she should quit, but he hasn't mentioned this lately. She looks out the window at the yellow leaves of the sycamore in the backyard and wonders what this means.

She finds him in his workroom at the back of the house. The smell of gun oil permeates the air. It is the very smell of fall for her, and of so many of the men she's known. Foster has always hunted, often with other boys who are grown men now, middle-aged, but weren't when they first took to the woods together and stood at deer stands, waiting to prove their worth and have their shirttails cut to mark a first kill, their faces bloodied.

He's sitting at a table sighting through a detached barrel, checking, she knows, to make sure the bore is clean. He's always taken care of his things. There have been times in their marriage when she's felt taken care of, too, but now the meaning of that phrase has changed, as if she's become a chore to him, a thing that has to be kept up, repaired. The last time they were intimate, two months ago, his every move was mechanical, a means to an end maybe less satisfying to him than the sight of a smooth bore and a well-blued barrel. And not any better for her.

"Are you all right?" he says and smiles. The smile makes him look boyish, despite his thinning hair and the lines at the corners of his mouth. There's something genuine about the smile. Maybe he's happy playing with his toys, she thinks, and then decides that perhaps she's being too hard on him.

"I'm tired," she says. "I don't know why people wait so long before they come in. Looks like some of them would rather have their teeth fall out than actually get help. And the ones that come in regularly think you're their shrink, and they want to tell you every secret about their lives."

He merely nods at first, his way, she knows, of reminding her that he's heard all this before. "Lucinda called a little while ago," he says. "She won't be coming home this weekend."

Their daughter is in her last year at the university in Tuscaloosa, and she's grown in ways Carrie couldn't have imagined. She's learned not one but two foreign languages, traveled overseas, and matured into a confident young woman.

"You were probably planning on hunting all weekend anyway," she says, backing away. "Who all are you going out with this time?" She hears the tone in her voice, but it's too late.

He looks up, not smiling now, in recognition of what lies behind her words and tone. He puts the barrel down on the table. "We haven't had this conversation in a long time."

"No," she says, "I guess we haven't."

He continues to gaze at her, as if he's curious about why she would approach the subject now. There is a reason, one she can't stop thinking about, but if he asks, she'll have to pretend otherwise.

She suspects he's had affairs. It would be easy enough for him, traveling from one job site to another in every little town within a forty mile radius: Linden, Greensboro, Demopolis, Livingston. Too many to name. If so, he's been smart about it, and chosen the women well. None have ever made their presence known to her in the subtle ways that would elude most husbands. All she knows for sure is that at some point he began to check out of their marriage. He became less attentive, less affectionate. She'd like to think the change came when Lucinda moved out, but she knows better. His turning away began much earlier, as he became more successful in his business and the money started to accumulate. At first he grew sure of himself in a way he never had been. She was happy to see the change, and was glad her money no longer had to feed them. But he grew beyond confident. He bought more expensive clothes, his truck no longer looked like a truck owned by a workingman, its paint job too pristine, and his shotguns and rifles bore engraved silver plates. The real difference, though, was in his touch. He became a different man, and she knows, thinks it now as she begins to prepare supper for the two of them, that any new man always wants a new woman's touch. Of course, his wanting may not have led to anything. She doesn't know for certain. She has no proof. Just as her father had no proof to offer weeks earlier when he told her what had really happened in those woods on that luckless November morning so many years past when her husband and the other young men with him decided to play war.

She and her father had been sitting on the back porch looking out at the overgrown pasture, and the far line of woods beyond held all the grays and browns and greens of brush strokes, but they did not transform themselves into anything more than they were, evergreens and hardwoods, not then.

"I don't know that he's going to leave you," he said, "and you don't neither. You want him to leave you? That what this conversation is really all about? You want him to do it so you don't have to?"

She couldn't answer. Maybe she did. He looked at her and she turned away from him and from the pasture and woods. She noticed the ornate planter by the back door, the one her mother had bought, held nothing but dirt, and cracks grew in its sides.

"If he's walked outside his marriage, it don't mean that has to be the end." He said this quietly, hesitantly. She knew why. It was the first time he'd ever come close to talking about what he'd once done to her mother. They had all known about it, as had most of Riverfield, and she'd watched her mother slowly forgive him. She wished now for her mother's strength, enough of it to make some kind of choice of her own.

She sees her father every other day and either cooks a meal for him or brings something she's already prepared. After her mother died from cancer three years ago, his health began to turn. He retired from the paper mill finally and the arthritis that had crept into his ankles and knees, like some damn thief he said, was the biggest reason. He could no longer stand on the cement floors long enough to complete a shift. When the stiffness and pain found its way into his hands, she took him to the doctor, and they found his blood pressure was so high that he had to be hospitalized. She saw, for perhaps the first time in her life, a look of fear in his features; not even when her mother died and he'd had to realize he would be alone, and probably for the rest of his life, had she seen such an expression.

During this period, though, their relationship had slowly deepened in a way she never would have expected when she was young. He had always been so distant from her, and often as cold as some November morning. It was her mother she'd continually turned to for comfort, reassurance. The loss of her mother left her feeling exposed to the world in a way she'd never imagined possible, and while she could now talk to her father, glad for the change in him, she found it ironic that he also appeared physically transformed into a man who only resembled his earlier self; even his very bone structure looked altered by his arthritis.

"But if he leaves me," she continued, not sure what she wanted to say. "You hear stories from women about husbands hiding their money. I don't know what his business is worth, what he might do or not do. I don't have to have the house, and I can work full time. But I don't want to be left with nothing. Sometimes I feel like he's a ghost around the house. He's already left me and all I see is what little of him he wants me to. It's like he's always had some secret. Now that Lucinda's grown and away at school, he wouldn't even have to pay me child support."

Her father looked toward her as if he had something to say. Often he didn't. So when she saw a tightness in his face, she knew to wait and listen. "There is something I don't guess he's ever told you. Never told me neither, but I heard about it from somebody who knows. If I was to tell you, I guess it would give you something, an advantage maybe. But maybe not. You might be afraid to use it. Maybe wouldn't want him to know you knew."

"Daddy," she said, tension, or fear, building within her, "go ahead."

"When that Tilghman boy was killed..."

"Bruce."

He nodded. "It didn't happen the way they all said. It wasn't a hunting accident."

"What are you telling me?" she said. She remembered Foster had come home that day dressed in camouflage, eyes downcast and dark beneath the shadow of his cap.

"They didn't see any deer at all that morning. So they decided to play a game, the six of them. They picked teams and made the rules."

She didn't follow him, wanted to interrupt, but made herself keep quiet, her body becoming more tense even, like a small woodland animal about to spring and run.

"Said they'd aim high above each other's heads, that they'd yell out *killed* before they pulled the trigger so each one of them could take turns falling down and playing dead, laying below the spray of buckshot. It was supposed to be just a game of war."

She sat in disbelief, recalling all that Foster had ever told her about that day. Four hunters, including Foster, had lined up on stands down in a creek bottom, maybe thirty yards apart, and the other two, Bruce and his younger brother Dale, had been the drivers. They'd come down through the bottom, yelling and hollering to scare any deer past the standers ready with their twelve-gauge shotguns. A buck had broken at the very last when they all thought nothing was in there. He moved so fast, and they all shot. Then another broke through the brush, a doe probably, and they kept firing, all six of them at the two deer, only one wasn't a deer and nobody knew or could say who'd shot Bruce in the chest and face.

But this wasn't what happened.

"They walked to the top of the creek bottom," her father said. "Three of them up one side, three up the other. Then they started toward each other. Whoever got to the top of the other side first, won."

"How were they going to know who got there first?" she asked, and then realized the question had no point.

"They had flags that they made up. It was whoever captured one of the flags first."

"Flags made out of what?"

"Their orange hunting vests."

Because they didn't want to be seen, she thought. They all took them off.

"Then there was a lot of shooting and yelling, and before they knew it, Bruce was down and wasn't getting up."

He stopped the telling then, but she wanted him to keep talking and somehow explain it in such a way that made things right. "Who did it?" she asked, quietly, afraid of the answer but finally having to ask.

"I don't know." He spoke the words so simply.

This wasn't what she'd expected to hear. "Who told you this? How did they know any of it?"

"Dale told me, years ago. He used to work under me at the paper mill, before they fired him, that is, and Foster gave him a job. I think he was having a hard time with it still, what they'd done, how they'd all agreed to cover it up."

"You don't think it was him, do you?"

"No, but I think he knows who. He wouldn't say. That was the one thing Dale kept to himself, said he had to. They all swore they would."

She looked toward the woods again and imagined men standing just inside the tree line with guns in their hands and blood across their shirts, their stares all on her. She squinted her eyes and that was when she was first able to see the trees as smears of color that transformed the world around her beyond anything she wanted to recognize.

As she drives to work early Friday morning—her uniform freshly washed, all her sterile instruments waiting on her, the monotonous music that has become a trial to her probably playing in each examining room—she keeps asking the questions that have been in her mind for weeks now. Could it have been Foster who shot Bruce, and was it his idea to play war? Was one any worse than the other? There's another question, too, one she first asked long ago, and keeps asking, and for which she's never received a satisfactory answer. She doesn't understand how Foster and the others can continue to carry guns into the woods and shoot what moves obscured through brush and trees, and that might fall into a human shape. This was the conversation Foster didn't want to have when she found him looking into the detached barrel. She thinks she has an idea now, though. Each was afraid after that awful day that if he quit hunting, he would look like the guilty party. And once they made that decision, they kept on, maybe hating to carry a gun into the woods. But Foster doesn't seem to hate it, she realizes—which could mean that he knows without doubt that he isn't the guilty party. The other alternative isn't one she wants to think about, but she does.

There is one silence she has kept herself all these years, and now it speaks loudly inside her mind, even while she works in the wet cavity of someone's mouth with her instruments, latex gloves, and the mask across her face. On a winter night, a Saturday, weeks before her marriage, she had straddled Bruce Tilghman in the cab of his truck while country music played on the radio. They were parked in one of the campsites down at The Landing on the Tennahpush River. She did it because she knew she had the power to, because he had always wanted her, and because she was the girl she had become, needing more than what little her father could give her, more than just her mother's reassurance, needing and then rejecting the attention of boys, and hadn't yet become the woman she is now, married, older, a mother, responsible for more than herself, understanding how much there is to lose by any empty and pointless indiscretion. She'd lost her virginity at The Landing, too, and had broken that boy's heart, just as she knew she would do the same to Bruce. He'd kept quiet, though, Bruce had. She was sure. But now, so many fears run through her mind that she finds it difficult to concentrate on almost any task, and sleep is as elusive as the dream she had for her life: a simple home, children, a husband who adored her and whom she could trust. A girl's dream, maybe. At least this is what she thinks her dream was.

She lies beside Foster at night listening to his quiet breathing—he's never snored—and wonders at what she did with Bruce, and at what Foster might have done if he had learned about that night down on the river. After they married, Foster kept up his friendship with Bruce as he always had, and they hunted together, sometimes just the two of them. She wonders, though. Maybe he didn't find out the truth until later. Maybe Bruce confessed it to him at some point and begged forgiveness, which he thought had been given him.

Her biggest question now is what to do with all she knows, and all she doesn't know.

That afternoon, she makes a trip to Riverfield, and just as she is no longer the girl she was, Riverfield is changed too. Old houses she knew as a child have burned or been torn down; the country stores where she bought Cokes and candy bars and picked up items for her mother are closed, empty, some of their roofs falling in—only the Bait Shop remains open, though it's no longer called that; pastures where cows once grazed are grown up in briers or covered in catfish ponds owned by people she doesn't know. The community she called herself a member of is transforming itself beyond recognition.

She means to pass her father's house, her destination a little farther on today, but Foster's truck, silver and black, sits there, as out of place as anything else in Riverfield nowadays. She cannot remember him ever going to her father's alone, but perhaps there have been times she hasn't known about. In case they might see her pass and ask questions later, she pulls into the drive and parks.

Foster comes through the door, surprise registering on his face. "Didn't think you were coming out here today."

"Decided I'd see Daddy this afternoon and give myself a break tomorrow." This isn't true, but the words come easily enough. "So what are you doing here?"

He looks at her as if trying to understand her question. "I been in Valhia, and when I came back through and saw your father out in his yard, I stopped. Am I not allowed?"

There is silence for a moment. "I'm sorry," she says finally. "It's just strange to see you here alone."

He stands on the steps still, looking down at her. "I've stopped before. I've always liked your father. Thought you knew that."

"All right," she says. "You headed home?"

"After I go by the office."

He looks as if he wants to say more but thinks better of it. Instead, he steps toward her, and for a moment she thinks he's about to kiss her quickly on the cheek. He doesn't. He simply passes beyond her.

Once inside, she can't help but ask her father what Foster wanted. He sits at the kitchen table while she begins to heat a frying pan and mixes cornmeal into batter.

"He just stopped," her father tells her. "He does that every once in a while."

She slows in her movements. "You didn't..." She can't make herself ask what she really wants to ask.

"Didn't what, Carrie?" For a few seconds the only sound is the crackle of batter poured into the frying pan's thin layer of corn oil. "Didn't tell him what I've known about Bruce's death and never told him before? Or that you want to leave him?"

"No, neither one," she says. "I know you wouldn't say anything. But didn't he come for some reason?"

Her father gets up from the table and walks out of the kitchen, his movement slow, unsure, as if the result of some outward injury, and not the spread of arthritis within.

She knew Foster would wake early, but didn't know that others would arrive before daylight. She hears them at the door, and is afraid there isn't time for her to make it back to the bedroom with her cup of coffee before Foster lets them into the house. She could remain in the kitchen, but she figures Foster will bring them in there where the lights are too bright and her nightgown thin, too revealing of herself.

She makes a choice and walks out into the living room, her arms crossed, the coffee cup in her right hand. Dale, always the polite one, looks away, and Foster doesn't seem to notice what she's wearing. Russell, who's worked for Foster for years, and was one of the six that day, looks at her as if she might begin to strip for him. She doesn't trust Russell, knows he's spent periods of time in the city and county jails for drunkenness, fighting. Finally he seems to realize that he's staring and turns away, though not as quickly as Dale. She is reminded of the power her body held when she was young, and of her willingness to use that power. Now she feels merely awkward, unsure how to move across the room, the way she should have felt, perhaps, as a teenage girl. Time feels reversed somehow, out of sync, as if these men in the room are still boys, two of them wanting her, one feigning indifference, and all of them capable of foolishness and stupidity to such a degree that no one can guess what they might do, least of all themselves.

"If you give me a minute," she says, "I can fix y'all some breakfast."

"I'm sure they've eaten already," Foster says. "And we need to load a few things and get moving."

Russell and Dale nod their heads, letting Foster speak for them, which is something she's noticed before but takes more note of now.

She goes into the bedroom and puts on her robe, closing it tight. She feels armored now and wants, or needs, to face the three of them again so she can stand there, no longer vulnerable. She quickly brushes her hair and wishes she had on makeup, but there isn't time, and besides, they've already seen her without it.

She enters the living room and hears them at the back of the house in Foster's workroom. He'll probably take them through the kitchen and out the side door, closer to where his truck is parked. She walks into the kitchen, feeling the cold tile against her bare feet. When they come in, Foster and Russell are carrying leather and canvas gun cases.

"Thought I'd let Russell borrow my new Marlin," he says.

"You bought another rifle?"

"A few months ago. A .30-30."

Dale stands there holding a cooler. He looks at her this time. It occurs to her that he's now older than his older brother. She can see some of Bruce in his features and imagines what Bruce would look like if he had lived. He'd probably still be wearing a beard, and it would hold at least as much hint of gray as Dale's. His narrow brown eyes might be more squinted, the skin around them sun hardened worse than Dale's. She realizes she's staring and turns away before she embarrasses him.

"Old Dale only got one deer last season," Foster says. "We're going to try to get him another one today."

"Figure I just had some bad luck last year," Dale manages.

"Either that or your eyesight's going. How many fingers am I holding up, Dale?" Russell says.

He laughs, or at least makes the attempt. "Six?"

"That's right. I've always had six fingers on my right hand."

"Where are y'all going?" Carrie asks, though she doesn't really want to know. It's just something to say.

"Down on the Black Fork," Foster says, "to that two hundred acres I bought last year. I got half a dozen tree stands built on it. Permanent ones, almost like penthouses." He laughs.

This has always been his answer to the question she's asked. Since that day, they no longer hunt by driving the deer past standers holding shotguns. Foster either hunts alone, or they all use tree stands and no more than three of them go at once. The answer has never satisfied her, and now, after her conversation with her father, it's even less satisfying.

There is one thing for which she gives him credit. He doesn't bait fields by putting out corn or planting winter grass.

Foster opens the side door and they file out behind him.

"Good luck," she says, because she feels she has to. Usually she adds, "And be careful." But not this time.

Dale is the last one out the door. He turns back and his eyes dart toward her and away, like some animal not daring to venture close enough to be fed by a human. She understands he doesn't want to go, and that his eyesight has nothing to do with why he killed only one deer last year. He has probably killed just enough to remain one of them and never questioned why he would do such a thing. She smiles, and he turns through the door, banging the ice chest against the doorframe. If she told him she'd been on her way to see him the day before, she guesses he might have slammed into the door's glass pane so hard it would have cracked.

Late that afternoon, she hears them in the drive, but Dale and Russell don't come inside. Foster carries both of his guns, each in its case, into the kitchen, where she stands to greet him. She isn't certain why she's there this time. In the past she was always waiting to see his face at the door, to determine at first glance if something had happened, again. She felt she was the only one who realized tragedy isn't limited by chance or by anyone's measure of the odds.

He tells her he killed a six-point, that they field dressed it, and took it to a processing place out on the highway for butchering. Some of the meat will be ground into sausage. She doesn't say it, but years ago, he would never have gone to one of those places, if they'd existed then. He took more pride in his hunting.

She asks about Dale and Russell, and when she hears that Dale killed a spike she feels a sense of disappointment whose depth surprises her—disappointment for him, and maybe in him.

✳

Then it's mid-week, late enough in the afternoon that the light is beginning to disappear, like the memory of a day not worth keeping. Too many days like that, she thinks, and turns onto the Loop Road, a narrow, gray-surfaced county road lined by barbed-wire fences, trailers and shacks, the occasional brick house. She follows the road to the far side of the Loop to avoid having to pass her father's house on the highway. After a few more minutes, she travels through a stretch of thick woods and tries to create an abstract vision of color out of their density, but she's passing too deep into the trunks of water oaks and the green fans of palmettos. They are all too close and starkly real.

Finally she sees, beyond a small pond, the brick house where Dale's parents have always lived. And not far from the pond, farther down, sits Dale's trailer, its sides still in good shape, not dirty or in disrepair. She knows she's cutting the time close, that he'll be home only if he left work right at quitting time and didn't stop anywhere. She is hoping to spot his truck, but it's not there, and after easing to a stop on the thin gravel, she decides to wait on his front steps.

Soon headlights sweep off the road and toward her, and she realizes just how quickly darkness is approaching. He parks beside her car and seems reluctant to get out of his truck, as if she must be waiting with bad news.

"I guess you didn't expect to see me when you got home," she says when he approaches.

He looks toward his parents' house a moment, then at her, and smiles. Maybe it's only a nervous smile, but she's glad to see it and leans to the side so he can walk up the steps beside her.

"I was over visiting Daddy this afternoon," she says as she stands, "and thought I'd stop by. When I come over I never take the time to go see anybody. Seems like nobody visits anymore."

"I reckon not," he says. "Don't have many visitors here, anyway."

"Can I come in, Dale? There's something I want to ask you about." She knows no matter how nervous she might make him that he'll let her in, and she knows why. The same wanting she sensed in his brother.

"The trailer's kind of a mess. We can sit out back," he says.

She follows him inside. A pile of clothes sits on the sofa, beer cans line the coffee table, and tools cover the kitchen counter. He opens a sliding glass door, turns on an outside light, and they walk onto a wooden deck. She understands now why he wants to sit outside. It isn't so much because of the mess inside. She can still see his parents' house from here, and they can see her if they care to keep watch and not wonder what a married woman might be up to in their son's place.

"I hear you killed a spike the other day," she says and sits in an old metal chair.

"Yeah." His tone is almost apologetic, and he doesn't look at her. He's waiting, she knows, and he won't make small talk, doesn't know how and doesn't want to learn. She admires this.

"You don't really like to hunt, do you, Dale?"

He looks at her now as if she has learned a secret he thought he'd kept well hidden. "Maybe not as much as some people. And maybe I'm just not as good at it."

The light that shines above him is from a yellow bulb, and it casts him in a pale hue that makes him appear jaundiced and, she's afraid, colors her perception of him. "Hard to be good at something when you don't like it," she says.

He only nods, not in agreement, it seems, but in recognition of why she's speaking to him as she is.

"You've always been smarter than you let on."

He smiles again, appears to appreciate the compliment.

"Dale, I know about the hunting accident," she says quietly and lets the words sink in. "I know what happened."

His smile leaves with the last of the natural light. "You're going to have to tell me what you mean," he says and looks away.

"I know y'all were playing war."

He waits, as if silence might erase what she just said. "How long have you known?"

"A while," she says and won't let herself say more.

"Why'd he tell you? He wasn't supposed to."

It takes a moment, but she understands that he's talking about Foster, and isn't sure if it's best to let him think this way or not. She wants to keep her father out of this, but Dale might decide to say something, ask Foster why he talked.

"He didn't tell me everything," she says. "And I couldn't bring myself to ask what I wanted to know. I didn't even know what to ask at first."

"I can guess what it was, but I can't tell you."

"You know who did it, though, don't you?"

"I didn't say that."

"Whose idea was it in the first place? Tell me that much at least."

"Why's that important? It was a stupid idea, but we all went along with it. We didn't know what was going to happen. It was an accident, maybe not like we told the sheriff, but an accident just the same."

He's looking out into the dark, as if it might provide some further answer that will satisfy her. The shape of the pond is just barely visible, but can't be mistaken yet for anything other than what it is.

"I don't think you believe that," she says. "You try to tell yourself it's just the same, but you know it's not."

"What are you wanting here, Carrie?"

"To find out what happened."

"Then talk to your husband. What I think is my business. He knows more than me."

"What does that mean?" she says and feels for the first time that maybe she can learn something from him. "Was it Foster's idea?"

He doesn't move or speak, but she can tell how much this is taking out of him. She hears a cow lowing at the edge of the pond, calling for her calf.

Dale finally leans forward. "It was Bruce's idea."

She wants to believe him, even thinks through the possibility, but knows it's a lie. She can't believe anything he tells her, not now. He needs time. She's surprised him too much, pushed too hard. She reaches out and takes his hand, holds it, feels its warmth, a working-man's strength in it. "I'm sorry, Dale. I'm not trying to do anything to hurt you." She gently squeezes his fingers. "After all, we've known each other all our lives. I've always cared about you. You know that."

He looks down at the boards beneath them and nods his head the way a boy might. She realizes what he wants her words to mean. A part of her counts on this, and another part truly does care.

"I know thinking about Bruce hurts. You must still miss him, and hate what happened."

He looks back up at her. "What about you?" he says and drops her hand from his. "I know you cared about him too, didn't you?"

Now he has surprised her, if she hears his words right and his question isn't a question. She looks toward the pond, and its still surface looks like an oddly flat section of pasture that cows might graze upon. "Of course," she says. "Everybody around here did. That's the way it was back then. People cared."

"Yeah," he says, "a long time ago. They'd spread rumors too, though."

"I guess they would, Dale," she says and thinks about her father and how public his affair became. She can only guess at the rumors Dale is hinting at, and she isn't going to ask. She's too afraid of what he might know, what Bruce could have confirmed for him. "Please don't tell Foster I came by. You're right. I need to ask him for answers, but I don't know if I can or not."

He doesn't answer her, or respond in any way she can see.

"Please, Dale. Don't say anything."

He finally nods. "Okay."

Stars begin to show themselves, and for a moment she feels as if their reflection on the water's surface has now turned the pond into an upside-down night sky full of sharp-finned fish.

At the end of the week she works until closing, then goes to see about her father. She avoids the subject of Foster, and her father seems relieved at his absence in their conversation. She says nothing of her visit with Dale.

When she returns home, she's grateful to see her daughter's restored '65 Mustang sitting in the drive. She finds Lucinda and Foster in the den, both of them on the sofa. Foster's back is to her, and Lucinda doesn't notice her at first. They seem to be discussing something important, and when Lucinda finally sees her, she stops talking in mid-sentence, as if the conversation between them can't be shared. Their bond is something that Carrie has always envied.

Lucinda rises, smiling, hugs her tightly, and she feels such relief in her daughter's embrace, in the very scent of her child.

"Mama, you've got to help me with Daddy," she says and stands before Carrie with a determined look, the same one she's shown the world since she was a toddler wanting a toy beyond reach. Her dark hair has grown longer, and what strikes Carrie most is how much more her daughter looks like a grown woman than the teenage girl who left home almost four years ago.

"So you're looking for an ally? Well, you should know I'm always on your side." She means to sound supportive, playful even, but when Foster looks up at her, she sees that he's heard it differently.

"Lucinda, go ahead and tell her," he says.

"Some friends of mine are planning a trip to Europe for the summer. A couple of them are the friends I went with before, and I want to go again. It could be my graduation gift."

Foster clearly isn't happy about the idea, which surprises Carrie. He has never held her back, always given Lucinda more than Carrie felt he should; it is a wonder that she didn't turn into a completely self-centered child, and Carrie likes to think she's responsible for her daughter's thoughtfulness. She was forever making Lucinda aware of other people's feelings, showing her how hard other families had to struggle. She couldn't stand by and let her daughter become what she had once been, though Carrie's own father had surely never done anything to indulge her.

A part of her wants to side against Foster, but she knows it's the worst part of herself. "That's an expensive trip," she says. "Most young people don't get to take trips like that right out of college. They've got student loans to pay and have to get right to work."

"I know," she says. "And I know I've already spent a semester in France, but since then I've learned both French and German. This trip could be good for me." Lucinda then adds that someone majoring in international business ought to go overseas, and not to just one foreign country.

When she hears her daughter name her accomplishments, Carrie is once again amazed and proud, and maybe what is most amazing to her is that she herself—who grew up sweating in her parents' garden, hoeing beans and picking peas to keep the grocery bill down, riding in pickups on dates with boys whose ambition was to farm with their daddies or get on at the paper mill or steam plant—a girl who never even thought about going to college, gave birth to a daughter who wants to see the world far beyond the pastures and woods that lie between the confines of the Black Fork and Tennahpush rivers.

"What you're saying does make some sense," she says and looks at Foster again. He shakes his head almost imperceptibly. "But your father and I will have to talk about it."

"All right," Lucinda says and then asks if she can help get supper ready.

"In a little while. You going out later?"

"Maybe."

She hears a solemn note in her daughter's voice as it trails off, and while it may come, in part, from having her plans for summer placed in doubt, Carrie also knows coming home feels strange to her now, her old friends distanced from her by time and by her own choices, ones that Carrie never felt she had or at least hadn't recognized.

Lucinda leaves the house after supper, and Carrie feels a sense of uneasiness as the sound of her daughter's Mustang fades. She'll have to talk to Foster now and find out why he wouldn't explain his objection to Lucinda. After her second-year semester overseas, which she'd had to have for her degree, he'd even mentioned the idea of her going back after graduating. She'd been the one against it, maybe because she felt his biggest motivation was so he could tell people he'd given her such an extravagant gift.

He comes into the bedroom while she's changing into a nightgown, and she hurries to slip the gown over her body. He doesn't speak at first but walks into the bathroom. She hears water running in the sink, and when he emerges, he's taken off his shirt. His chest is still muscular and a portion of dark hair remains among the gray.

"So what's your problem with her going overseas? I'm the one who hated to see her little girl go over there."

"She's not a little girl anymore."

"Exactly," she says and sits on the edge of the bed. "And there sure aren't many fathers who'd say that."

"I'm different from most fathers."

"Maybe that's why she loves you so much."

He looks at her, smiles for a moment, but she can see he doesn't want to talk about this.

"I'm not saying I'm all for it, but it could be a good thing for her," she says, "help her get a job. You've even talked about it."

"I think maybe you're right. It's time for her to go to work." He pulls off his jeans and sits across from her in his boxers.

"That's not exactly what I said. There's something you're not telling me." She thinks then that there is a lot he's not telling her.

"It's just not a good time." He pauses, seems to search for the right words. "I may have to lay a few people off. I was going to have to tell you at some point, might as well be now."

"Why? Lay them off for good?"

"You know what the price of gas is like."

"What's that got to do with anything?"

He appears irritated now, as if he's about to explain something he shouldn't have to. "Oil has gone sky high. Asphalt's made from petroleum, and my costs are up something terrible. My bids on jobs haven't been low enough, and all the towns I've done business with aren't wanting to spend so much money on their streets. They just don't have it to spend."

"Why haven't you told me before now?" She watches his expression harden. "You don't think it's my business?"

"I didn't say that, or think it. Don't put words in my mouth."

"You just bought a new rifle. And the land you bought along the river? You don't mind spending money on yourself still."

"The rifle wasn't that much, and the land was before things started getting bad."

"How bad are they?"

"Bad enough where I'll have to say no to my daughter, and now I've got to fire people."

"Not Dale?" she asks and is surprised at how afraid she feels for him.

"No," he says and looks away. Then he adds, more quietly, "Never Dale." The inherent question calls her back to that creek bottom she never actually saw but from which she'd escaped for a little while when she first saw her daughter's car in the drive.

Early Monday morning, she drives just ahead of Lucinda, who is on her way back to school. After they make the interstate, they leave the Black Belt behind, and the landscape turns bland and monotonous. Carrie feels she could be anywhere. At first the feeling of distance is welcome, but finally she feels she is simply no place at all.

Her father is riding with Lucinda so they can visit. Carrie can't remember ever taking a trip alone with him, and she wonders what he and Lucinda talk about. It seems her daughter has always understood the men in their family better than she has. And maybe having a granddaughter who crawled into his lap as a child is what first began to open up her father to the grown daughter who gave him such a gift.

Last night she'd sat with Lucinda and told her she would talk to Foster again about the summer trip. "I'm not making you any promises. He may not listen to me. A trip like you want would cost thousands, and that might be too expensive right now. He doesn't want me to tell you this, but his business is down."

"Is that why things don't seem quite right between y'all?"

For a moment she was surprised by the question, but she knew she shouldn't have been. Lucinda had always been perceptive. "If things seem a little strained between us, that's probably why."

Lucinda looked at her with the kind of compassion that Carrie hoped she had helped create. "Then he's been having money problems for a long time now, hasn't he?"

She looked down at her daughter's open suitcase on the floor and was finally able to say no, but she offered no other explanation, and thankfully her daughter seemed to accept her silence.

Carrie pulls into the parking lot of the doctor's office now and Lucinda follows. Her grandfather has to take his time getting out of the small car, and Carrie sees him struggle to hide his pain. Lucinda hugs him—careful, Carrie notices, not to upset his balance. And despite the fact that Carrie visits her father every few days and knows the shape he is in, witnessing his physical deterioration yet again makes her feel unbalanced herself.

"Thank you, Granddaddy," Lucinda says, and Carrie guesses that he has slipped her some spending money. She wonders how much. Whatever the amount, it has to be more than he ever gave Carrie, but she's glad that her father can do this now. It's one of the few ways in which some men his age can show love to a daughter or granddaughter.

"When will you be back?" Carrie asks. The bright morning sun is in her eyes, and she has to squint to see.

"I don't know. I'll call." She hugs her mother good-bye, and, after a moment, Carrie watches her pull into the stream of morning traffic flashing past.

Inside, she and her father wait. He is here to see his rheumatologist. There are only two other people waiting, older women, and they sit near each other across the room. Like all doctor's offices, the place smells faintly of ammonia and beneath that the hard-to-define smell which somehow hints at sickness and age.

"I could have driven myself," her father says.

"You could have, but I know how hard on you it is to drive this far. I don't mind doing it."

They sit in silence for a few minutes, the only sound the kind of lazy droning music she hears at work while scraping a patient's teeth. She's trying to decide if she should talk to her father about Foster, and realizes that he is really the only person she can talk to about him. She wonders when her life became so shut off, when she stopped having friends. In a quiet voice she tells him what's happening with Foster's business and what Lucinda wants for the summer. He nods and doesn't speak.

"You act like you already knew. Did Lucinda tell you?"

"Yeah." He turns more fully toward her. "But I knew about Foster's problem before she told me."

"What? Why is it that you know so much more about my husband than I do?"

One of the older women looks toward her.

"I'm sorry," he says. "I didn't feel right about keeping it from you. That's why I'm telling you now. But it was his place to tell you, not mine."

"With all I've told you about the shape of our marriage and what I'm afraid might happen to it, you should have told me what you knew a month ago."

"I didn't know then."

Both the old women are now reading magazines, or at least pretending to. "When did you know?" she asks.

For a moment he doesn't answer. "The day you saw him at my house. That's when he told me."

"I knew there was something going on that day. But why did he tell you? It's not like you were going to loan him any money."

A nurse comes out and calls a name Carrie doesn't hear clearly. One of the women slowly stands and walks toward the nurse.

"That's not why he was there. I called and asked him to come by."

"For what?"

"It had to do with Dale."

"How is that?" she says. "Seems like everything here lately has to do with Dale."

Her father gives her a puzzled look. "Dale comes and talks to me sometime. Has ever since we worked together."

"He like some son you've always wanted?"

"No, Carrie. He just needs a little advice every once in a while. Sometime you can't go to family."

"So what's his problem?"

"It looked like he was going to lose his trailer. He missed some payments and didn't want his folks to know. So he asked Foster for help. Whenever Dale's needed money over the years, Foster's given it to him. And I don't mean a loan. He's given it, and pretty regular."

She starts to ask why, but the sick feeling in her stomach tells her she already knows, and it confirms all of her fears. "Foster wouldn't give it to him this time, would he?"

"No, he wouldn't. So I talked to Foster for him. He still wouldn't. That's when he told me things weren't going good with his business. I didn't know whether to believe him or not."

"But he went hunting with Foster after that. They were at the house together. Things seemed fine between them."

"Things ain't always what they seem. And he can't really tell Foster no, can he? Even if it's just to go hunting. Foster's his boss."

"Some people could say no."

"Well, Dale ain't one of them. And you know Dale well enough to know that much."

"Foster could have given him the money," she says. "The business may be down, but Foster's got money in the bank."

"I figured that. But maybe he doesn't have as much as me and you think, or figures he's paid Dale enough by now."

She's quiet for a moment. The soft music and her father's voice begin to fall away. How much would be enough? Just how large is Foster's debt? she wonders. Then her father's name is called. He stands and finds his balance. She's ready to rise from her chair and catch him should he begin to fall.

That evening, before she leaves work, she approaches one of the doctors, the older of the two partners. She knows that Diane, a woman she's worked with for several years, is going to take maternity leave; Diane and her husband are expecting a first child. Maybe she'll come back to work, maybe not. Carrie asks the doctor if he would consider letting her work full time, maybe permanently. He seems genuinely surprised by her request, as if he thinks she must have some great need for the extra money. She doesn't try to explain that the money is only a part of her reason for asking, that maybe just as important is her need to stay occupied, and to stay away from her husband.

At home, she's anxious about telling Foster. At first she tries to convince herself her anxiety exists simply because Foster will be irritated, say she's overreacted to the news about his business.

They eat a too-quiet supper, and then he leaves her for the den to read the paper or watch television. When she finally enters the room, he's paging through an old hunting magazine, either too bored with what it offers or unable for some reason to concentrate on printed words. She sits down on the sofa and tells him what she's decided, tries to make it sound as if she only wants to help cover the loss of a coworker.

"So did you go and ask for the extra hours?" he says and closes the magazine, drops it beside his chair. "The business isn't in such bad shape that you've got to do this. You think I can't take care of you?"

"Who's to say I need taking care of? And no, I didn't ask. Hadn't thought about it, but when he offered, I thought *why not?*"

He waits a moment before answering. "You sure you don't have some reason of your own for doing it?"

Now she tenses, recognizes why she was so anxious. It wasn't because he might think she overreacted. She was afraid that her working more would show her hand to him too soon, let him know that she wants to separate herself from him, wants some way to provide for herself.

"Like what?" she says.

"Like coming up with some money for Lucinda to go to Europe?"

"No," she says, relieved. "I hadn't thought about that." Then it seems that maybe the thought should have occurred to her. But her own life is important too, she thinks, not just Lucinda's.

She begins working the longer days, and on Saturday she sleeps late. Foster has been gone for hours. He is quail hunting with the mayor of Valhia somewhere on the mayor's farm. Foster doesn't like him, says he's the kind of man who'd shoot quail on the ground if he thought no one was watching. It's business, he told her.

At some point during the day she will need to check on her father, but that can wait until later. She showers, slips into jeans and a green blouse that's cut a little lower than what she usually wears. She puts on her makeup, careful not to apply too much, and then touches more perfume to her neck and behind each ear than she would for a social occasion. When she looks in the mirror a final time she knows she appears attractive for a woman in her late forties, but she can't say she's happy about what she sees, and the scent of her perfume smells like some flower that's maybe too common to be valued.

She thinks of calling first, or even coming up with a pretext that would bring him to her house, but either would scare him. She will have to go there, curious parents or not, and hope, again, that he's home or shows up soon.

After crossing the bridge over the Back Fork, she drives onto the low ground of her girlhood and remembers who she was and knows she's about to call on a part of that old self who must be in her still. But she has a deeper understanding now, a clearer judgment of what she is and isn't capable of, what she should and shouldn't do. Or maybe words such as *understanding* and *judgment* are poor substitutions, she thinks, for what is really a more studied shrewdness. It may be she's not changed at all if she can set out on such an undertaking as this.

She knows she could simply leave her husband, walk away into a life of her own, and one that she *could* own, no matter the cost. But after twenty-five years of marriage she feels she's earned a larger due, and maybe most important is the right to know if she married a man who can take aim at another man and kill him as if he were a deer trying to survive hunting season in stark November woods.

As soon as she turns off the Loop, she sees his truck parked in front of his trailer. She doesn't honk her horn the way some buddy of his might, someone like Russell. Instead she climbs the steps and knocks on the door. He doesn't answer, or won't. The day is clear but windy and cool, and she wants to close her jacket but needs him to fully notice her, to be surprised by what he sees standing at his door, wanting inside. She knocks again.

Then she hears her name called from a distance, the sound of it reduced by the wind, and turns toward the voice. Dale stands in front of his parents' house, waving her over. This isn't what she expected. She's unsure what to do, but she knows his parents, can make conversation with them.

The wind ripples the pond's surface, and roan-colored cows stand beyond it. He waits patiently as she approaches and doesn't seem surprised to see her, though he must be.

"I was beginning to wonder if you were anywhere around," she says. "Are your parents inside?"

He shakes his head at first, as if he doesn't want to speak. "They went up to Tuscaloosa to see Alabama play Ole Miss." The wind blows his hair and she sees how fine it is, streaks of it a lighter brown than she realized.

"You didn't want to go?"

"I'll listen to it on the radio after a while. Where's Foster at?" he says, and she can tell the question isn't as casual as he'd like for it to sound.

"I'm just over to see about Daddy, and Foster's quail hunting."

He looks around like he's not sure what to do next. Then for the first time she sees his eyes stop on her and take in her figure. He asks if she wants to come in and get out of the wind.

She's never been inside the house. The living and dining rooms are better furnished than what she expected, and there's a graceful sense of design and muted color. Then she notices a table filled with family photographs and sees, for the first time in more than twenty years, a picture of Bruce. It makes him real for her again in a way she couldn't have guessed. The image of the smiling, bearded young man only a few years out of high school forces her to remember the way he felt up against her body in the cold cab of his truck, his trimmed beard on her exposed skin. He isn't just gone away, she thinks, disappeared. He's dead, still, with holes torn all over his face and chest.

"Sometimes I look at that picture too," Dale says, standing beside her now. "I forget it's there." He pauses a moment. "Then I see it all over again."

The way he says it makes her wonder if he means something more than the photograph.

"That happens to me with pictures of my mother," she says.

He nods. "I was about to make a sandwich in the kitchen when I saw you through the window."

"I'll make one for you," she says, impulsively, "if you'll get everything out." She can see that he's not sure what to make of her offer. And she knows he's waiting, like before, for her to say why she's come.

He leads the way into the kitchen and goes to the refrigerator, hands her packages of lunchmeat and cheese, a jar of mustard. She takes off her jacket and begins working at the counter and can sense him behind her, watching. She wonders if he's imagining that this is what it might feel like to be married with a home, a caring wife taking time for a simple task to please her husband. She wishes he had that. Then wishes she did, that she could be that kind of wife again, to someone.

They sit at the kitchen table, framed by a large picture window that looks out on a broad pasture. Sunlight pours in, and she knows what the light does to the sheer fabric of her blouse. They are mostly quiet while he eats, and then she gets up to pour more sweet tea in his glass. She walks up behind him and slowly leans over his shoulder with the pitcher, the scent of her perfume strong enough still so that she sees him take a deep breath and hold it. She imagines his eyes are closed.

"Does this house still feel like home?" she says when she sits down.

"Mostly. I come over here a good bit, and eat here a lot. But I've lived in town, too. I just like it better out here."

"Is it about money?" she says. She watches him closely. He stops chewing for a moment, then swallows.

"It's cheaper, if that's what you mean." He takes a drink of his tea, keeps looking at her over the top of the glass. "I don't have to pay rent for a lot to park my trailer on."

"Do you still owe on the trailer?"

He looks out at the pasture. "I guess you been talking to your husband after all, huh?"

"No," she says, suddenly not sure what to say; the way he said the words *your husband* sounded strange. "Not about what *we* talked about, the shooting, I mean. But…"

"About my asking him for a loan. I'd asked him before for help. So I asked again." He stops talking and shakes his head, and she sees more hurt than anger in his eyes and face. "I would of paid it back," he says, and now she hears, sees, only anger, and it seems to run deep, as if its real source lies buried within him.

She decides to remain quiet about what she learned from her father. She'll let Dale think what he will. "Things are a little tight," she says but doesn't tell him that Foster will soon lay off some of the people Dale works with. She feels, in her silence, a level of disloyalty toward him.

"I'm sorry," he says, though she's not sure why he's apologizing. "I'm caught up now. It's okay."

She nods, doesn't ask where the money came from but imagines his parents. Or it could have come from her father, she realizes. He wouldn't have told her that part if it had.

He finishes his sandwich and she takes the plate, carries it to the sink and cleans up. When she's finished she turns to him, sees that he's been watching her. "I'm going to go find a bathroom," she says and walks out of the kitchen.

"Down the hall," he calls from behind, and she keeps walking as though she has been here many times before and knows already where it is.

She finds it, takes her time, and checks her makeup in the mirror that Bruce must have stood before long ago and sees then a glimpse of the girl Bruce had finally known. She turns away, not satisfied with what she saw of herself, but resigned.

He'll come looking for her in a few minutes. She's farther down the hall, figures the master bedroom is at the far end. And of the two rooms across from each other, where she's now standing, one of them has to have been Dale's. She spies a large desk through the doorway to her left, metal file cabinets beyond the cluttered oak desktop. Then she walks to the doorway of the other room. A double bed, neatly made, hugs the far wall, a dresser sits next to it, two model jet planes on thin pedestals look as if they are arrested in the midst of take-off. She imagines Dale dreaming of mid-air adventures as a boy, and teenage fantasies about local girls, including herself, that followed.

She hears his quiet footsteps on the hall carpet but continues looking into the room and out a window. A lone pickup travels the Loop, its muffler too loud. He steps inside the doorframe, so close that her body feels aware of him. He doesn't speak.

"I was curious," she says. "Do you mind?"

"Curious about what?"

She turns to him, and though she felt it already, is still surprised by his closeness to her in the narrow space. "Curious about the house, the room you grew up in," she says. "Do you ever sleep here?"

He looks at her as if puzzled by the question. "No," he says, but she isn't sure that he doesn't.

"Did you make those model planes?"

He laughs quietly. "Fighter jets," he says. "They're not exactly models. Me and Bruce used to build them from kits. They're the only two left. Mama kept those, said we couldn't tear up everything she bought us. We used to put them together, then go out and fly them, shoot each other down and crash them into walls, or the ocean." He smiles. "No telling how many are still laying on the bottom of that pond."

He's describing pleasant boyhood memories, smiling, but what she hears is something different, as if his words are altered by the time that's passed since those planes fell and crashed. "Playing war," she thinks and realizes she's said the words aloud.

His smile fades and, even though the hall and doorway are dimly lit, she sees him more clearly than she did in that circle of jaundiced light on his back porch. His eyes are narrowed in a painful reflex, and she guesses his sight has turned inward, aimed on a moment so deeply real that he could never have imagined it. Her questions leave her mind; she doesn't want his answers now but simply to place her arms around his shoulders, around the boy he was, and to offer him more than she ever gave to Bruce. She touches him, whispers *I'm sorry.* The fabric of his shirt smells like broom sedge that was carried on the wind, and she feels as if she's at the edge of some other, abstract place.

When she arrives home, Foster is in the backyard cleaning quail. He will fry them for supper, fix a whole meal for the two of them. The thing she will most dislike about eating the quail is biting into the small pellets of birdshot and dropping them beside her plate.

Later, he'll reach for her in the dark and she will turn away.

The next days pass quickly with her longer working hours and the shortening of time that always comes with late fall days, robbing the afternoons of their light. One evening Foster tells her he has let go two employees, both young men who are single, uneducated, but shouldn't have a hard time finding other manual labor. Then he surprises her. "I thought about letting Russell go too," he says. "Wish I could." He tells her Russell doesn't work as hard as he used to, that he sometimes doesn't show up for work, says he's too unpredictable. Someone younger would work harder, and cheaper. "Why didn't you let him go?" she asks, ready to weigh his response. He doesn't offer any other reason than their friendship. And she feels now the friendship is bound together by an artificial means that Foster can't explain without damning himself.

✳

The long dirt road is rutted, in worse shape than she ever remembers. The ruts shake her car until she feels the vibration within herself and slows. She crosses a set of railroad tracks and sees open fields on either side, then large sections of closely planted pines growing toward harvest, and finally thick hardwoods. Long ago, she most often traveled this road late at night.

Her phone had rung that morning, and when she saw the name on the ID screen, she wasn't sure what to think. Dale asked if she was driving over to see her father since it was a Saturday, said he'd like to see her. His voice was halting and he told her his parents were home. From his long pause afterward she knew he wanted to meet somewhere other than his trailer.

From the top of a rise she sees the muddy Tennahpush and the cement boat ramp that angles into it. One truck with an empty trailer behind sits parked in the asphalt lot. This time of year The Landing is usually deserted. Instead of parking she turns right and weaves her way through the trees on the narrow road that is asphalt now also but wasn't when she was a teenager. Foster's company did the work. She passes camping spaces and catches flashes of the river through the woods. Finally she reaches the sharp point of land formed between the Tennahpush and a large creek that empties into the river. Dale's truck sits at the farthest camp space.

He walks over to the cement picnic table and she joins him there, sits down next to him on the table top. They don't speak at first. She looks at several camp spaces on the other side of the turnaround and knows that one of them was where she told Bruce to take her. She wonders if Dale knows this.

"I didn't know if calling was the right thing or not," he says.

"It's all right. I'm glad you did."

They are both silent again. The only sound is the wind threading through the trees after passing over and catching the chill off the river. She waits for Dale, and keeps waiting.

"Doesn't look like I have much to talk about," he says.

"Dale, tell me something. Did Bruce ever tell you what happened between us?"

He looks out at the water, as if he's trying to remember. "No, he didn't. But I always knew he had a thing for you."

She isn't sure she can believe him, but she doesn't push. "Guess I've said too much then."

"It's all right. If you mean what I think you do, I'm glad he had that. I mean you. I mean. . ."

She touches his shoulder and he turns quiet. "I know what you're trying to say. Thank you." She sees then the tilt of his head and a certain tension in his face. "It was before I got married," she adds, anticipating him.

He nods, and then surprises her. "But were you already seeing Foster?"

The question doesn't sound mean, but she wonders. "You could say that. Yes."

He seems to study what he's heard. "You didn't want anybody to know. Didn't want Bruce talking about it."

"No, I didn't." Now she pushes. Believes it's finally time. "Do you think he did? You think he might have told somebody? Maybe. . ."

What she sees in his expression might be surprise or mock surprise. "You're afraid he told Foster. That's what you're worried about. Or you think Foster found out and. . . Lord."

They are both quiet again. She turns toward the woods and half closes her eyes, looking for some pattern of odd shapes or colors into which she can disappear for a moment.

"Do you think Foster could have shot Bruce on purpose?"

He appears genuinely puzzled. "Why do you want to think Foster did it?"

"I don't. I'm just afraid."

He remains still, looks into the woods as if they are a passage back to that time and place, then shakes his head. "I'm sorry. And don't take that to mean anything about Foster either way. You know, it wasn't just three of us there. It was six."

"Meaning what?"

"It could have been any of us, and we all swore we'd protect each other."

"Decided that none of you would talk about it, right? But Foster finally told me," she says, ventures the lie to see what it might gain her. "He broke the promise."

"I know, and seems like his being the one to tell you about it would tell you something else—that maybe he ain't the one who did it. Because if he was, why would he bring it up?"

She isn't sure how to respond. The more they talk it seems the more difficult the puzzle becomes, and her lie didn't help. "You know, Dale, when I first asked you about this, I never said that it was Foster who told me. You just assumed it was." She pushes herself now. "The truth is, it wasn't him."

He looks at her as if he can't believe what she's said. "Who else could have told you? The other two who were there don't live anywhere around here. Gavin's down in Florida. Judson's in Memphis. They were the smart ones. They finally just got out."

She's about to tell him who else, but he looks away, remains silent. "You tell me," she says softly.

"I'd almost forgot." He still can't face her. "Your daddy?"

She doesn't want to embarrass him, make him ashamed. But she can't stop now. "So you're the one who broke the promise."

He shakes his head, not in denial but as if he can't believe what he did. "That was years and years ago. I had to talk to somebody. I couldn't sleep. Could hardly do my work."

"Dale," she says, "it's all right." She places her arm around his waist. "You were the youngest out there. It was your brother. You knew you could trust my father."

"So can I trust you?" he says.

She moves closer to him and slides her hand up his back and over his shoulder. "Of course," she says, her mouth close to his ear.

He's already turning toward her, and she sees such need in his eyes, so much that she feels a moment of panic for what she's done, about to do. He's closer now, his eyes closed. Then she feels his mouth against hers, the slight coarseness of his beard. She pulls away, pushes him back, not hard but with force enough. "No," she says, not sure if it's in true answer to his question or to his advance and need of her.

"Why not?" he says. "It almost happened when you came to the house."

"I know it did."

"Did you not want it to?"

She isn't sure how to answer. "I think I might have."

"And now?" he says.

"It wouldn't be right, and would complicate everything."

"Then why did you come to the house? Why are you here now?"

"I just... Dale, I..."

"You just want to know what happened. That's all." He turns from her, stares out at the water. The wind picks up and she sees the side of his face harden against it, or against her. "You can't help it, can you? That's what Bruce told me. He forgave you. Said you just couldn't help yourself."

"So he did tell you," she says. "And he must have told you where, seeing as how it was your idea to come here."

He turns completely away now, shows nothing of himself to her. "Have you not changed at all?" he says finally.

She closes her eyes, shakes her head, and feels something drain out of herself, as if she's received an injury meant for her long ago but can't yet tell where on her body the wound has appeared.

Her mother is who she needs most now, and in some ways she still can't believe, even after five years, that her mother is gone from the world. At times Carrie can hear her voice, the warmth and softness of it, the two of them sitting in the kitchen in Riverfield while a roast cooks in the oven or her mother rests just before mopping the floor. Sometimes the conversations are remembered; other times imagined, as now, while she sits in her own kitchen. Do I leave him? she thinks, then hears, *I didn't leave.* The memory of ammonia in mop water is so real it stings her eyes and nose. *But that doesn't mean you shouldn't.*

And then comes the question Dale spoke and that keeps echoing in her mind. *We all change, honey,* her mother says from somewhere just beyond the open kitchen door, *but not always in the ways we want.*

Mid-week, and she's last to leave the office parking lot. After she cranks her car, headlights shine across her windows, truck headlights. She sinks inside, not ready to face him again, not expecting she would have to, not for some time at least. Then the muscles within her chest tighten, as though someone has burst into her vision from out of a nearby patch of trees. Russell is walking straight toward her.

She considers driving away. His truck doesn't have her blocked in, but she waits, rolls down her window. Maybe something's happened to Foster, but she doubts it.

He leans down quickly, places both hands on the door, his thick fingers just inside her window. "Guess you went to him 'cause you thought he'd be easier to handle than me. You shouldn't of messed with him the way you did." She looks ahead, doesn't answer. He straightens for a moment, his crotch level with the bottom of the widow. Then he leans back down, his face closer to hers this time. "You listening to me?"

She doesn't answer.

"You really got him rattled. You think that was a good idea?"

"I only wanted to talk. I knew it wasn't easy for him."

"Now we're going to have to talk, but not here where people might see."

She thinks about driving off again but decides it would only delay the inevitable. So she follows him to the highway. The Mississippi state line is twenty-five miles away, but they're not going that far. Just past the city-limit sign sits on old apartment complex. Number eleven, he told her. She doesn't think she knows anyone else who lives there, though someone could recognize her. She's glad it's dark, but can still see how rundown the buildings appear. She parks and waits for him to go inside. He doesn't turn on the light above his door, and in a few minutes she enters without knocking, which makes her feel strange, as if she's stepping into the familiar.

He's sitting on a sofa with a bottle of beer in his hands. The place is neater than she expected, but the furniture is as worn as the brown carpet that always seems to cover the floor of every cheap apartment she's ever been inside. He sees her looking around. "The ex-wife got all the nice stuff," he says. "Have a seat."

She takes a chair near his end of the sofa and holds her purse tight against her hip.

"I ain't said nothing about any of this to Foster yet. Maybe you can think of that as a favor to you."

"All right, I will," she says. "So what exactly did Dale say to you?"

"That ought to be pretty clear. You just need to leave him alone. He knows he best not tell you what you want to know. And if you keep taking yourself to him, you going to make things hard for him."

"Sounds like you're threatening both of us."

He shakes his head slowly, drinks from his beer. "You don't get it. I wouldn't ever do anything to Dale myself. I wouldn't have to."

"What's that mean?"

"Never mind. I'm trying to help him. That's why I'm talking to you. Truth is, I think you're a bitch for what you did, the way you came on to him."

"I didn't," she says.

"Yeah, you did. You picked him instead of me, and we both know why."

"And why's that?" She pushes farther back into the chair and wishes she hadn't sat this close to him. He's stronger than her, and angry. The door's not locked, she remembers, and tries to tell herself there is no reason to feel fear.

"'Cause I'd have your clothes off before you knew what hit you. And you know what would happen after that."

She stares at him, not surprised by what he's said but disgusted. "Not in a million years. And listen to who's coming on to the wife of his oldest friend."

He keeps his eyes locked on hers, lifts his beer, then turns away for the quickest of moments before turning back. "You know he's fucked around on you. Just like you did to him before you got married."

His words are a punch she wasn't expecting. She absorbs it and the hurt as best she can, but is most struck at how the truth of something she was already certain of could still be so powerful. "And that's supposed to make some difference here, between us?"

"I'm just saying."

"I know what you're saying, and it tells me what kind of man you are."

"What's that? The kind who could shoot somebody out in the middle of the woods? Or is that the kind of man Foster is?"

"You tell me."

He laughs, shakes his head.

A new tactic occurs to her. "Why'd your wife leave you, Russell? She figure out the 'kind of man' you are? She know some answers about what happened in those woods? Maybe I ought to talk to her."

He doesn't speak at first but lowers his head toward his chest, as if he's having trouble breathing and needs to regain his breath and some deeper part of himself, maybe say some kind of prayer and ask for strength. "Not only does she not want to talk to me," he says and drinks from his beer again, looks around the room as though for something lost, "she don't even want to talk *about* me, not with anybody." He looks up at her. "So if you're trying to threaten me now, you going to have to come up with a better plan than that."

"How long have y'all been divorced?" She's not sure why she's asking, unless it's some distant sadness on her part at the thought of any marriage ending, and her own so close.

"I don't want to talk about her anymore. She don't know about this. And you just need to stay the hell away from Dale."

"I know that," she says and waits for him to respond.

"Maybe so, but my guess is you're going to keep on until you hurt him or somebody else even more. Mark my words. I don't know that I can live with that."

She stands and faces him.

"Seems like you've already got more hurt than you can live with. All of you. Maybe somebody ought to tell the truth."

He glares back at her. "Just remember, it ain't yours to tell."

She almost responds but instead walks to the door, out into the cold night air, and thinks how true those words might be.

Light shines through several windows. She wonders how long Foster has been home, and is afraid it's been long enough for him to want to know where she's been.

She finds dirty dishes in the sink that he must have used to heat leftovers. Then she hears water running through pipes and realizes he's taking a shower. She eats from a small plate of cold roast and not much else. The food is tasteless and the thin streaks of congealed grease manage to make her slightly sick.

When she enters the bedroom he's standing beside the bed, a towel wrapped around his body, his hair still damp. "Sorry I'm late," she says. "I went to a baby shower for Diane, from work."

"You must not have stayed too long," he says, which surprises her. "How come?"

She can't tell if there is doubt in his voice. What she thinks she might hear may be in her own mind. "Just wanted to come on home."

He turns from her and walks to his dresser. When he pulls away the towel and drapes it over his shoulder, she realizes she can't remember when she last saw him standing naked in front of her, even as casually as this. She imagines some other woman has, though, but not at all casually. He pulls on a pair of boxers. When he turns toward her again, he doesn't meet her eyes. It's as if he can't, or doesn't want to. She wonders what he might know, if maybe Dale has finally said something to him. She half expects him to turn on her now, demanding to know just what the hell she thinks she's been doing. She feels sicker and the queasiness spreads through her body. He goes over to the closet and pulls out a dark shirt, slips it on with deliberate movements. She has no idea what he's thinking, or what to say to him.

"Won't be long before Lucinda's home." Her words sound feeble to her. "The semester's about over."

"Maybe we'll see her before then."

He steps close to her, his shirt hanging open, his chest and stomach partially exposed. "Aren't you going to change out of your work clothes?"

"I guess."

"Or are you just waiting for me to leave the room first?"

She doesn't expect this, but perhaps shouldn't be surprised. What does surprise her is how troubled, not angry, his words sound. They're heavy enough to push her down to the edge of the bed, and she sits with her head lowered for a moment. She takes her shoes off and without speaking begins to unbutton her top, then quits, looks up at him.

"If you really want, I'll leave you alone," he says. "If it's come to that."

"No. There's no reason you should have to leave." She finishes with the buttons and pulls off one side of her top. He sits then, and she lets him help her with the rest of it. She finally stands and slips out of the white slacks, then feels his warm hand at the small of her back, feels his fingers slide just beneath the waistband of her underwear.

It's been months, but she feels no desire, or even need, for him. All she wants is to change clothes, alone, but he's here, wanting her, and maybe she has some need she can't quite name and looks down at him just as she did earlier with Russell. Except now she places her hands on Foster's shoulders and pushes him away, feels a sense of strength in her arms as she does, and in what she's about to ask him.

"Have you ever cheated on me?"

He doesn't look away or act surprised. It's as if he has expected such a question, been ready for it. "No," he says. "I haven't." And then: "Have you?"

She isn't ready for the question, but she answers as best she can. If he doubts her he doesn't show it. Or perhaps he dealt with the question of her fidelity long ago and laid it to rest with the greatest of finalities, and was then free of it.

She moves slowly towards him, maybe only out of a need to prove with the deception of flesh that she's never been unfaithful, or maybe more out of a need to reduce him to his most base self, and to meet him there in that place of shame familiar to them both. She climbs onto his body not unlike she did with Bruce, and even further back to the very first boy whose heart she broke, but there is no pleasure, only a practiced motion, a knowledge of necessary movement buried in the center of her muscles. And in her mind, or heart, the opposite of what a wife should want to feel for the man she married and whose child she bore.

Moments afterward, his body quiet, hers still atop his, he looks up at her. "Am I so terrible?"

"I don't know," she says, then sees in his expression what can only be the purest of hurt.

The grocery store is crowded with people shopping after work, but she pushes her way through, bumping first one cart, then another with her own. Later, when she enters her father's house carrying heavily laden plastic bags, she sees right away something is wrong.

"I'm sorry," she says. "I know it's been a few days. I missed coming yesterday and should have called."

She carries the bags to the kitchen, and when she walks back into the living room, he turns the television off with the remote. "Just as well you didn't. If you'd come, I'd of probably still had company."

"Who?" she asks.

"Shouldn't be hard for you to figure out."

"Dale," she says quietly, answering the way a child might while suffering a scolding.

"No. Try again."

She knows, this time. "Russell."

"That's right. And he told me some things. Why in the world would you go to Dale? What I said to you was between us, for you to use against Foster only if you had to. That son of a bitch Russell shows up here last night and threatens me, tells me to keep my mouth shut. And no telling what Dale thinks of me now. He used to trust me. I should never have told you what I did. I shouldn't have trusted you."

She sits down across from him and looks at him sitting there, a walking cane at his side, his body shaped by age and arthritis, but his words to her, the disappointment in them, reshape him again into the father she remembers. "I let Dale think it was Foster who told me."

"But that didn't last."

"No, it didn't," she says. "What happened with Russell?"

"I threw him out, that's what."

"Do you think he's dangerous? You think he's the one who did it, shot Bruce?"

"I don't know. I think he's scared, and I think you sure created a mess. No way Foster ain't going to find out about all this."

"I don't think he knows yet," she says.

"So what are you going to do? If Foster comes to me, I'll have to tell him the truth."

She leans forward in her chair, as if she might be sick. "You won't say why you told me about Bruce, that I might leave him? Foster, I mean."

"Might? Make up your mind, Carrie. And no, I won't tell him why I told you what I did, but he'll want to know. You can count on that."

She knows she has to do something, that she holds people's lives in her small grasp, maybe not unlike someone in November woods with his fingers wrapped around the stock and trigger of a shotgun. But where to take aim?

"You still haven't told me why you went to Dale."

"To find out what happened and what kind of man I've been married to."

"You didn't want Dale for some other reason?" He's studying her carefully now. She knows what he's asking.

"No other reason," she says. He looks away from her, shakes his head at the brevity of her answer, as if he doesn't understand her, or doesn't want to. Sitting there, in her father's house, she feels she is still the girl she used to be and tried to leave behind. Maybe everyone's greatest sorrow is that they can't escape the worst of themselves, but whatever she might acknowledge within her, she knows she has to look beyond it now, past its bone-gray color and abstract shape.

Her father calls her name, and she waits for any further condemnation she can gather from his words, prepares herself for it. "Carrie," he says, and appears to grimace with arthritis pain, "it was Foster's idea to play war."

She follows the unlined blacktop, lets it carry her back on the arc of its curve, her headlights picking up just enough of the road in front of her so she can find her way. Then she turns onto gravel, follows the beam of her lights and the sound her front tires create on the small rocks beneath their treads. She catches the flash and reflection of lights across a still surface and imagines small planes breaking that surface, descending into wreckage, sharp-finned fish navigating among them.

Dale's trailer is as dark as the pond water. His truck isn't there. Lights shine from his parents' house, though, and she sees their vehicles. For a moment she feels relief, and then her anxiety grows larger. She knows she has to make herself face him. She begins to turn around in front of the trailer, but stops, feels compelled to get out of her car, and tries the door. It's unlocked. She isn't surprised. Its being left open seems the act of someone who doesn't care. There's a light switch beside the door, she remembers, and finds it under her palm. His parents, she knows, might see the light come on and wonder, but maybe she doesn't care.

The trailer is filled with as much disarray as before. She manages to locate a note pad beside his phone and writes the simplest words she can, *I'm sorry. I need to see you*, and then signs it, just her name, which seems cold to her, the same kind of cold brevity as in the answer she gave her father, but she doesn't know what else to write.

When she pulls away from the trailer, she sees a lone silhouette move forward in front of his parents' house. There is no porch light on, and she can't tell if the figure is male or female. She doesn't stop; she accelerates, gravel ricocheting off the undercarriage of her car like sprays of lead pellets.

She's afraid to go home, scared of what may, or may not, be waiting on her, but she crosses the Black Fork, follows the highway that threads the river's connected pools of backwater. When she parks in her drive, she sees that Foster isn't home. It's as if this absence is what she anticipated, and she now divines some connecting logic in the two absences that makes her more afraid.

Once inside, the house feels empty, hollowed out of something more than belongings, and holds no note of explanation left on a counter for her. She then checks her cell phone, sees her daughter tried to call. There is only one message. "Dale didn't come in today," he says, "didn't call. And his parents haven't seen him." He tells her he may be late, that he's going to go look for him. His voice doesn't sound particularly worried or upset, and she doesn't detect any anger or suspicion. If he finds him, though, what will he come home knowing?

She doesn't sleep, or if she does it comes without her knowledge and leaves with only a hint that it was taken from her. At a little past midnight, she hears him enter the house. She remains still, quiet, listens to his movements, then feels the bed give with his weight.

"I found him."

"Where?"

"Across the river," he says, his voice still low. "At Duff's Place."

"He all right?"

"Drunk as I've ever seen him. People said he showed up like that. I took him home and he passed out on the way."

"I'm glad you found him," she says. All she can think about is how they could have come to the trailer while she was there and wonders what she might have said. Then she remembers the note, her name signed at the bottom, like some confession.

"Go back to sleep," he says.

She can't, but in the morning she'll wake and find him gone.

At work she tries to stay focused. She pushes tongues out of the way, uses the small round mirror to search for build-up on molars and bicuspids, but she wanders into strange places, openings in her mind that don't seem to contain reason, and she imagines the hurtful words and lies these mouths have spoken to wives, husbands, lovers. She knows her patients, knows something about the lives they lead, the divorces, the abuse suffered, the cheating. She thinks that no mouth is ever really clean, that a human bite almost always infects.

At lunch she tries to call her daughter but gets no answer. Then she checks her voicemail, sees there's one message, and hopes for the sound of Dale's voice, realizes how badly she needs to hear it, and this need feels like a good thing to her, something hopeful in itself.

"Saw your note," she hears. "Don't know if Foster did. He could have." His voice is flat, cold even. "You do what you want. I'm here."

She supposes she deserves the words of punishment, but then she realizes the punishment was more in the sound of his voice than in the words themselves. Or perhaps what she heard lay beyond punishment, was something deeper, more troubling.

The afternoon passes slowly, and finally darkness closes against the small window near the ceiling of her examining room. She pulls on her long coat, buttons it against the cold that will be waiting on her. She wishes she could go home and change out of her work clothes, but there isn't time. She leaves the parking lot before everyone else, drives well above the posted speed limit.

She ends up having to sit and wait so long she cranks the car and runs the heater for warmth. Then she hears a vehicle behind her and turns her head, sees his truck. He parks near her, and by the time he opens the door to his apartment, she's beside him, startles him with her sudden presence, which she intends.

"What?" he says, blocking his doorway. "Foster got to you already?"

His question throws her. "No," she says, then pushes ahead. "I came to tell you to stay out of my father's house. Don't think you can threaten him to save your sorry self."

"You still don't understand," he says, and she follows him inside where they stand in the living room, each squared against the other.

"Just stay away. He doesn't need trouble from you. And if you want me to understand things, start talking."

"Far as I can see, you the one that brought the trouble. And as for me doing any talking"—he leans toward her and she smells some hard scent on him she can't name—"I decided it was time for that already, after the drunk Dale went on. I sat down in Foster's office this afternoon, and from the look of you a minute ago, I figured he'd already found you."

It's happened. Foster knows, she thinks, is bound to come at her now with what she set in motion. But how hard? "What did he say?"

"Didn't say a fucking word, but looked like he had plenty on his mind."

"Just how much did you tell him?"

"You ask him."

"Why'd you do it?"

"Dale," he says.

She shakes her head, knows further talk with him is useless, then walks out the door, imagines that very soon she may have to live in one of these apartments, call it home.

She stands in the cold and finds her keys at the bottom of her purse, hears the sound of people talking in the parking lot and pays it no mind. But the voices stop, all at once, and when she looks up she sees two young women whose faces she recognizes, and her daughter stands between them, looking at her as if she has just seen her mother step out of a motel room, one of those new places on the highway at the other end of town, where locals, it's rumored, take rooms on the back side that faces away from the highway. She has the odd feeling that somehow this is what's happened, that her daughter now knows some sordid truth about her that she didn't know before.

"What are you doing here?" she asks before her daughter can.

Lucinda doesn't seem able to regain a sense of herself. "I tried to call you. Decided I…was going to come home, so I just came on. Thought I'd stop and see friends, before I went to the house."

The two girls look from one to the other, as if something needs to be figured out before they should speak. She knows their names, Mary Kay and Barbara. The prettier of the two, Barbara, has finished college, and she knows that Mary Kay left for college too, but didn't leave for long. It is probably Mary Kay who lives in one of these buildings, works at some small office for little pay.

"How are you girls?" she asks.

"Fine," they answer, their voices too soft, as if they're afraid of intruding on some situation.

She looks at her daughter again. "I'm kind of in the middle of something," she says. "Trying to help an old friend. I'll see you tonight, won't I?"

"I'll be there, I guess." Lucinda doesn't sound sure, though, as if she thinks something has changed at their home, something she might not want to see, or perhaps Carrie is imagining that her own fears also belong to her daughter who can only make guesses about her mother's life.

"Tell your father what I said, will you? If he's there."

Lucinda nods slowly, more puzzled now, it seems. "All right."

She wants to say more, wants to put Lucinda at ease, but knows she can't and walks away, perhaps too abruptly.

After she starts her car, she lets the engine warm and turns on the heater. She looks in the rearview mirror, watches her daughter and her friends walk beyond the corner of a building and disappear, and imagines for a moment she is that age again. Imagination gives way to memory and she is newly married, starting her life with Foster in their own apartment. No daughter yet. Bruce is still alive. Then Foster comes home from a day of hunting down inside a creek bottom.

She waits for traffic to pass before she pulls onto the highway. Her cell rings, and she pulls it from her purse, determined to answer, to be somehow accountable to whatever voice she hears.

"I thought I would of seen you by now."

"I'm coming right this minute," she says. "I promise. I had to talk to Russell, but I'm on my way."

He doesn't respond to the mention of Russell's name, doesn't say anything. Lets only the quiet speak.

"Dale? Are you drinking?"

"A little. Enough."

"What do you mean 'enough'?"

He's quiet again, at first. "I'm glad it's you who's coming. Not somebody else. But I'm sorry for that too."

Someone pulls up behind her, their lights on bright, and she edges her car out of the way. When she opens her window and waves the driver around, she sees that it's Lucinda who passes, watching her, and has to be wondering what her mother is doing, who she is talking to, who she's seen, just as she wonders now why Lucinda is leaving so quickly. Then her daughter is gone, her red taillights melting into the highway's flow of traffic.

"Dale?" she says, finding her way back into the conversation. "Sorry for what? You don't have anything to apologize for. It's me who's sorry. More than I can say."

"It's all right. It doesn't matter. Nothing does."

"I'll be there in just a little while. Okay? I'll hurry."

"You don't have to. Hurrying won't matter either."

"Dale," she says again, waits to see if he's still there. She pulls onto the highway and the small beeps that signal call ended sound in her ear.

After she crosses the river, and the closer she gets to home, the more aware she becomes of the woods on either side of the road. It is as if the lines of woods are growing closer to the blacktop, edging in at her, and while they are more nearly shadows of woods in her vision than actual woods, more an abstraction of themselves than anything that might be considered real, the lack of color—no green smears of pines and cedars, no strokes of rusts and yellow-browns—strips her of the ability to create anything out of them within her imagination. Instead she feels entered farther and farther into their branches and thick trunks.

No porch light is on at his trailer, only a patina of light glows against an end window. His truck is there, parked askew. She knocks on his door, though she doesn't expect him to answer. She's certain the door will be unlocked, as before, and just as certain that she'll find him inside, though she is apprehensive now, a little afraid of the emotional state he may have crawled into, worse even than what she heard on the phone.

She walks into the dark, calls his name, and waits while her eyes adjust and she begins to see vague shapes around her. "Dale," she calls again. Dim light creates a passage down the one short hallway, and she follows it into what must be his bedroom. The bed she finds is unmade, and the light she followed bends itself into a wall, or the opening in a wall, and she supposes it's the bathroom.

"Dale?"

She doesn't hear any kind of answer but enters the doorway. What she sees startles her. He's half submerged in water, his bare knees bent at wide angles just above the tub's sides. The shower curtain is gathered toward one end, and she can't see his face or any part of his head or shoulders. His body appears severed. She takes another step closer, afraid of what she'll have to face, but the water's surface isn't sanguine; its depths aren't stained. She sees what she can't help but see, a thickness of brown hair and his shriveled penis. The pale nakedness of his body makes her feel as if he's lain bare in a manner beyond the physical. He moves, closes his knees enough so that neither of them will have to be embarrassed by his body, and she sees a small rectangle of metal on the side of the tub, not the old-fashioned two-sided blade her father once used, but the sort of blade workmen use for scraping, only one side honed sharp.

"I couldn't do it," he says. "I thought I could." His voice is quiet but distorted by the shape and finish of the tub and shower walls, but what she hears, while altered, sounds uncorrupted somehow.

Before she tries to speak, she lowers the commode lid and sits facing him so that she can finally see his face. He looks down at himself, though, pulls his legs up closer to his chest, and wraps his arms around them.

"I'm glad, Dale. No one wants to lose you. Losing your brother was too much already."

"That's right. It was too much. Worse for me than anybody, even my parents."

"I know," she says, and she does now.

"I can't live with it, or with myself. I don't know how. Even after all this time."

"But you are living with it. You do."

He looks up at her, his eyes resting in her vision beneath the hard ceiling light. "How is this living?"

"It's like everybody. Everybody's carrying around more than they think they can handle."

"Not like me."

"I guess that's true enough. Do your parents know?"

"They know what I could stand to tell them, and what I didn't tell anybody else. But they don't know we were playing war. I don't think they could forgive that, to know that's how it come about."

"You didn't ever tell my father?"

He shakes his head. "I told him the playing war part, just him. I shouldn't of done that. But telling my folks the worst part, and your father the other, it was almost like telling it all, except it wasn't."

"No," she says, "it wasn't. But playing war, that wasn't your idea."

"No." He looks at her again, waits.

"It was Foster's."

He nods.

"Dale, I know the water is getting cold. Let me get you a towel. Would that be all right?"

"Please," he says quietly.

She stands and reaches for a faded blue towel from a shelf and hands it to him while he rises, neither of them embarrassed now by anything as trivial as flesh. He wraps it around himself, and when she offers her hand, he takes it, steps out of the tub. She pulls him close and feels the wet skin of his back and shoulder blades against her hands, and his chest soaks her clothes, but she holds him tighter. "I'm sorry," she says, "for how I kept pushing you until..." She can't say the words, and she wonders how Dale ever spoke even a part of the truth to his parents, and to her father.

He responds only by letting her go. She knows he can't see anything beyond his own hurt. He walks out of the bathroom ahead of her, and she looks down for a moment, picks up the blade off the side of the tub and closes her hand against it, hard enough to feel its thin edge against her palm, right to the point of cutting into the folds of her skin and across her lifeline.

She leaves him in his bedroom to let him dress and stands beside the clutter of his kitchen counter, trying to decide what she should do. The idea of walking him over to his parents' house occurs to her. She knows she can't leave him alone, and she can't stay with him all night. There is really only one choice, and she knows it must be the right one because it's the hardest for her. She picks up Dale's phone and sees her note still lying beside it.

When she hears him answer, she quietly speaks his name.

"Where are you?" he says, his voice harsh. "I know where you been. Where are you now?"

"I'm at Dale's." She pauses, and then says all she can say. "He needs you."

She expects a hesitation on his part, but he says, "I'll be right there," so quickly it surprises her. It's as if he's been anticipating such a grave summons, and for a moment she finds herself hurt by how suddenly he responded, as if whatever anger he held toward her no longer mattered, and she no longer mattered. She cradles the receiver, lets it go, wonders if he has already let go of her.

Dale walks out of his bedroom in jeans and a shirt, his hair combed wet. He turns on the ceiling light but won't quite face her.

"I called Foster. He'll be here soon." He nods his head as though it's what he thought she might do, as if perhaps Foster is playing out his part in the way Dale expects, a way Foster has done before.

She sits on the small sofa, pushes a pile of clothes out of the way. "Sit with me while we wait," she says. "Please."

He finds room for himself, and the cushions sink, pushing them against each other. She takes his hand in both of hers and his skin is warm. "You can talk or not," she says. "It doesn't matter. Whatever you need."

He gently squeezes her hand, and she remains quiet, leans her shoulder deeper against his, and in her mind the images of what happened that day come clear, begin to play themselves out in slowed motion and in silence, perhaps the same way they've played themselves out in Dale's mind, and in dreams from which he can't awake but remembers in brutal detail so vivid as to be beyond real. Her husband moves through the trees and brush and leans down over the body, then finally pulls Dale away. And they stand talking, all of them, Dale no longer in tears but in a numb shock, listening as best he can while Foster tells them all what they will do, each of them nodding in turn, thankful for every word they hear, but resentful too in ways they don't understand yet because they have not lived with him, have not grown into men or into their lives the way she has now, with him and with their child, waiting for him to arrive and play out his part in front of the two of them who sit here beside each other and who can listen, or not.

Dale still doesn't speak; he simply waits. She would like to tell him it wasn't his fault, but she can't. She can't blame it all on Foster.

In a little while she hears him approach. When his truck door slams shut, she experiences a jarring inside herself, and she wants to rise and meet him but Dale still holds her hand, squeezes tighter, and before she can stand, he's there, inside the door, his coat open, his face reddened from the cold, his hair blown out of place.

He's quiet at first, calm. He looks at Dale, then finally at her, walks toward them and kneels down in front of Dale, which strikes her as odd, makes her unsure of what he might do. He places a forearm across Dale's knee, and she sees a gentleness in him that surprises her at first, but also sees that Dale isn't surprised. "How bad is it this time?" he says.

"Pretty bad, as bad as before. You know. When…"

Foster nods. "That's been a long time now. I thought you made me a promise after that."

"I know. I did."

"Is that why you didn't call me this time? Why you called Carrie instead?" He looks at her for a moment, and the look is not gentle but accusing and reminds her of what she faced from Russell.

"I guess," Dale says.

"It's okay. I'm here now. We'll talk this through. Okay?" He stands and looks at her. "I want to talk with him alone, if you don't mind too much."

"You want me to leave?"

"No," he says. "Just give us a little time. Wait in your car, or my truck. My key's in it, and you can run the heater."

She lets go of Dale's hand, pushes herself up from the sofa, angry at being told what to do, but doesn't want to remain where she isn't wanted. And it could be that it's best for Dale this way. She doesn't want to second guess what might help him.

Foster opens the door for her, follows her onto the small porch. The air feels colder, sharper. "Do you see what you've done?" he says in a low voice. "What you've pushed him to. My God, Carrie."

"What *I've* done?" she says, but he doesn't respond, merely turns and steps back inside, closes the door.

She goes to her car, cranks it, and thinks of leaving, but she doesn't. She knows she has a part in this too. After the engine warms she turns on the heat, lets it blow against her fingers and into her face until her skin feels it might burn. She wonders what Foster is telling Dale, or asking, maybe even demanding.

The outside light over the porch flicks on, and she watches for Foster to emerge, to signal for her to come back inside. She finally twists off the ignition, pulls her coat tight around her, and gets out of the car. They made this, she thinks. It belongs to them. I wasn't there, didn't pull a trigger or tell anyone what to do.

She walks out into the dark, no destination in mind. Soon she's aware of the flat surface and the reflected light of the moon and walks along its edge, imagines the two boys who fished here, waded out as far as they dared, trying to ignore the warnings they'd heard about water moccasins. She wonders how deep the water is, how far down lies the wreckage of wings and engines and small fuselages covered in mud and silt, such strange and unnatural objects for the sharp-finned fish that hover and glide through them, the water their air, the world above nothing that they have to contend with, only the world's wreckage that floats down to them. But those boys who walked out of this pond did have a world with which to contend; grown older they turned from play to other desires that grew in them and couldn't be let go like some toy plane thrown into the air. They carried guns together and shared a desire she had to contend with, but instead played with in the worst possible ways until she left one satisfied on the bank of a river and the other carrying both knowledge of that night and his own desire still, and maybe jealousy. She can't push the notion away any longer and wonders if Dale could have been carrying that jealousy along with him down in a creek bottom when he saw his older brother creeping among the trees. Maybe it spoke to him in a way he didn't understand or even realize he heard. But she doesn't want to think this, doesn't want to see his need for her all these years later as any kind of sign for what might have happened long ago in those late November woods. She reaches into her pocket, pulls out the razor blade, and pitches it into the water where it makes such a small sound against the surface.

The slam of a truck door carries across the pasture to her. He'll have to come to her, she decides, will have to find her where she stands. He calls, and she doesn't answer. He calls again, his voice rising until the last syllable of her name, that long vowel sound, thins across the cold air.

He turns slowly, searches every degree of the dark, and then must see her, or some semblance of her silhouette, and begins to walk toward her. He takes his time, and she lets him, doesn't move his way, even takes a few steps closer to the water, and waits.

When he reaches her, his hands are plunged deep into his coat pockets, his arms drawn close to his body, and she stands in much the same attitude.

"How is he?" she says.

"What do you think, Carrie? Not good at all. You think I can work a miracle with him in twenty minutes time?" He lets his words hang, then keeps at her. "The damage you've done to him."

"You think this is my fault? Sounds like it isn't the first time he's tried this. And it might not be the last."

"I know that."

"So was it my fault before—when I had no idea what had *really* happened but you never told me anything but a lie?"

He waits before he answers, seems to study the water and the dark for something he can say. "We all promised to tell the same story, and stick with it. I had to keep my promise."

"No," she says. "You *made* them promise. I know you. You handled it all."

He turns away from her for a moment. "That's been a long time ago now."

"Not to Dale, or to me either. It's all pretty brand new to me."

"According to Russell, you've known a while."

"Not that long."

"How do you think it makes me feel, you sneaking around asking people about me? And what exactly were you trying to find out from Dale? You just had to hear all the awful details, wanted to think the worst of your husband."

"Maybe I wanted to find out if my husband had killed somebody."

"*Killed somebody.* You say that like I could have murdered Bruce."

"It crossed my mind," she says too quickly, without considering how it sounds or what his reaction will be.

He faces her more squarely now, the wind catching his open coat.

"Why would you think such a thing?"

She can't search his face in the dark, can't see enough of it to judge what he might have known about her, and Bruce, and wants to hear her admit now. And he can't see her face, can't judge her the way he might want. The darkness, like their last attempt at intimacy, is evasion.

"I don't know. When I found out what happened, it seemed like *anything* was possible, and the worst I could imagine felt like what must be the truth."

Beyond her husband, she sees movement, a shadow approaching Dale's trailer, then realizes it isn't one person, but two, walking in slow step with one another. She watches them reach the porch and disappear inside. "You called his parents," she says.

"Right before I walked out here. He didn't want me to, but I did."

"How much more will he tell them?"

"I don't know. That's up to him."

"Is it? You really think that?"

"He's a grown man, Carrie."

"No. I'm sorry to say so, but he's not, and you know it. I think you've even counted on it."

"That's a hell of a thing to say to me. I did make the call, and told him he could tell them whatever he needed to."

"So you gave him permission after all this time. But you're betting he won't do it."

"I'm not betting anything. Maybe I'm scared, though. That what you want to hear?"

She faces the water again, sees the reflected light ripple along its surface with each gust of wind. "Why'd you make him keep hunting all those years, make him kill?"

She sees him shake his head, as if she can't understand any part of him or what happened. "He went with us, but he didn't really hunt, just carried a gun that he wouldn't even load. We'd kill one for him every once in a while, tell people he killed it, when he'd let us."

"And you think you did that to protect him?" He won't answer, and she doesn't blame him. "I know it was your idea."

"What?"

"To play war."

A car passes out on the Loop, and the loud bass thump of an indistinguishable song rattles and punctuates the air with concussive sound.

"Yeah, it was my idea. You're right. It was just something to do, something to pass the time, maybe to play at being men, soldiers. I don't know. I always wanted to tell you."

"No way do I believe that."

"That's up to you. But before you go any further, let me ask you something. What if he'd done it?"

She's confused for a moment, caught between the past and the present, between a shotgun blast and the slice of a razor blade, between the blood of two brothers pooled in equal measure. "Done what?" she says, but she understands him now.

"What if you'd found him dead in that tub?"

She glances at the water and then out into the dark just as he had a few moments ago, as if the darkness could provide what one of them, if not the other, might need. All the abstractions of color and shape she could once create are gone now. "I guess I would have reached in to see if he was still alive, to see if I could save him." She knows this isn't an answer to his question but is simply another evasion.

"Yeah," he says, "and his blood would have been all over you too."

She imagines her arms in the water, her sleeves soaked. She doesn't speak, nor does he. There's a long silence, and she feels a balanced quietness. She can't move, can't do or say anything that might destroy the even divide between them. But she knows they can't remain where they stand, hands in pockets, arms stiff at their sides.

It's the calling of their names that makes them break apart. She turns first and sees Dale's father standing on the porch, waiting on them. They begin walking, Foster a step behind, and she keeps moving ahead. Dale's mother appears, and Carrie wonders what they know. As she and Foster cover ground, approach the cast of the porch light, the couple look first at her, then behind at Foster, and back at her again. It's as if they can't decide who should claim more of their attention, or scrutiny. Carrie wants to walk or drive away, but what she shares with Foster holds her there, prepares her for whatever they have to face, though she knows it won't be enough to keep them joined.

PUBLICATION NOTES

THESE STORIES, SOME IN SLIGHTLY DIFFERENT FORM, were first published in the following journals: "Pasture Art" in *Shenandoah*; "Braided Leather" in *OCHO*; "Into Silence" in the *Sewanee Review*; "Haints at Noon" in *New Letters* and reprinted in *Redux*; "Midnight Shift" in *Louisiana Literature*; "Watching Kaylie" in *New Madrid*; "Playing War" in *failbetter.com*. "Short Days, Dog Days" was included in the anthology *The Shoe Burnin': Stories of Southern Soul*, and "Into Silence" was also published in *The Best American Short Stories 2010*.

ACKNOWLEDGMENTS

FOR THEIR SUPPORT AND ADVICE, I would like to thank my wife Rhonda Goff Barton, Jim Gilbert, and Kirk Curnutt. Thanks also to Betsy Teter for giving this collection a home. The books *Weren't No Good Times: Personal Accounts of Slavery in Alabama*, edited by Horace Randall Williams, and *Gabr'l Blow Sof': Sumter County, Alabama Slave Narratives*, edited by Alan Brown and David Taylor, were helpful in the writing of the short story "Haints at Noon."

HUB CITY
PRESS

HUB CITY PRESS is a non-profit independent press in Spartanburg, SC, that publishes well-crafted, high-quality works by new and established authors, with an emphasis on the Southern experience. We are committed to high-caliber novels, short stories, poetry, plays, memoir, and works emphasizing regional culture and history. We are particularly interested in books with a strong sense of place.

Hub City Press is an imprint of the non-profit Hub City Writers Project, founded in 1995 to foster a sense of community through the literary arts. Our metaphor of organization purposely looks backward to the nineteenth century when Spartanburg was known as the "hub city," a place where railroads converged and departed.

RECENT HUB CITY PRESS FICTION

The Whiskey Baron • Jon Sealy

In the Garden of Stone • Susan Tekulve

The Iguana Tree • Michel Stone

Mercy Creek • Matt Matthews

My Only Sunshine • Lou Dischler

Expecting Goodness & Other Stories • C. Michael Curtis, editor

Through the Pale Door • Brian Ray